By the Rivers
of Babylon

By the Rivers of Babylon

KHALID KISHTAINY

QUARTET BOOKS

First published in 2008 by
Quartet Books Limited
A member of the Namara Group
27 Goodge Street
London WIT 2LD

A catalogue record for this book
is available from the British Library

ISBN   978 0 7043 7126 2

Typeset by Antony Gray
Printed and bound in Great Britain by
T J International Ltd, Padstow, Cornwall

❧ Contents ❧

Honour and Dishonour

'Please, brother, remember what the Holy Koran says about mercy and forgiveness. "Forgive ye those who repent." She is only a child, barely seventeen. Keep her in the *kushik* room upstairs. Let her live on bread and water until God opens a way for her. It won't be long,' said Aunt Wafiah to Abu Mamduh, the merchant and horse dealer, at his home in the al-Mishahdah district of south Baghdad. She was one of the eight women – aunts, nieces and cousins – sitting on the elongated velvet cushions stretched out on the straw mats lying in the *iwan*, the spacious alcove of this oriental house with its central courtyard, the *haush*, open to the sky above. In one corner of the *iwan* stood a heavily decorated table of Indian origin, a rather unusual item in a Baghdadi house. The mahogany table held a brass vase, also Indian in style, with elaborate decoration. In the entrance hall, the *majaz*, there was the collection of shoes and sandals, fifteen in all, and one crutch, heaped together. Women must not desecrate the house with their shoes; only men were allowed that privilege. The entire house smelled of incense, mixed faintly with the odours of the lavatory and the septic tank, with its open round hole some four centimetres in diameter. A couple of famished stray cats, more like rats than cats, were sitting patiently upright, waiting for the ghost of a chance to raid the kitchen and help themselves to whatever was kosher for cats and happened to be left unguarded.

The ageing and old women were mostly dressed in black or dark navy, with the exception of Aunt Wahida and Cousin Sadiqa who wore simple dresses with florid patterns down to their ankles. But all the women had their hair, a mixture of black, brown and grey, wrapped in black *hijabs*, *futas* or *boyamas*, the traditional headgear of the middle-class women of Iraq at the time of the present story, the 1940s. They all gathered at this house of Haj Nufal Abu Mamduh and formed a theatrical semi-circle around him in the *iwan* with the sole purpose of sparing the life of Samira, the wayward teenage daughter. He was dressed in the traditional costume of a bazaar merchant – a long, flowing *saya*, gathered around his pot belly with a wide decorative belt, and a contemporary jacket, a remnant of the past and a hint of the modern, thereby portraying the true character of the Middle East as a mercurial mixture of ancient history and present-day *comme-il-faut*. Another piece of modernity was the pair of Saxone shoes worn with long socks which he kept in position with a pair of suspenders just below the knees. On his head, he sported the *imamah* of an old-fashioned businessman of his generation, consisting of two parts: a fez, the colour of a ripened pomegranate, enveloped by an embroidered cloth. The embroidery was the colour of gilt, signifying ill-gotten riches, yet enhancing the prestige and respectability of his rather long face, shaved but adorned with carefully trimmed moustaches dyed with henna, almost echoing the colour of the fez above. His ageing skin was scattered with a few spots, old cuts and traces of old Baghdad boils. As the women were speaking to him, he was toying with a thirty-three-bead amber rosary, at variance with the ninety-nine-bead black rosary prescribed for women. This was the only thing in which women were allowed to have more than men. But the male folk were allowed to choose any colour for the rosary, usually amber, real or fake, whereas the fairer sex could have only black rosaries and without the silver motif on the *shahul* bead.

Haj Nufal was not a Baghdadi nor did he make his money in the Iraqi capital. He was a trader in Basra in the business of exporting Arabian horses to his Jewish partners in India. However, he did not make his money from Arabian horses but rather from Indian women. The economic depression of the thirties had dealt a heavy blow to the racing companies in Bombay and Haj Nufal had to sell his thoroughbred horses at terrible losses. He did not know what to do and could not face the prospect of going back to his native town a penniless beggar. Prestige is all that matters to an Arab gentleman. He looked around to see what else he could do. It did not take him long to discover that there was more money to be made out of women than out of horses. With that simple discovery, he opened a small private brothel in Bombay, at first with just two fair women from Kashmir. The number soon increased to six and then to ten. A few months later, he opened a second brothel in Karachi. The business prospered and the 'Hajji' made quite a name for himself in most of the major cities of India.

Having accumulated enough money to impress his fellow men in Basra, he returned proudly to his home town, Iraq's only harbour, but his reception was rather cool. 'Aren't you ashamed to do that sort of thing? Haj Nufal al-Basri of the noble tribe of Hanifi engaged in pimping?'

'Why,' he answered his critics placidly. 'What have I got to do with it? A dirty Indian willie goes into a dirty Indian cunt, fick fock, fick fock – and I make two rupees out of it! What have you got against that?'

Yet Haj Nufal knew that the God-fearing people of Basra wouldn't understand his cool rationale and early sense of globalisation. He gathered his wealth and his family and moved to Baghdad where the people had a better understanding of this kind of business. Yet, he found the competition too stiff for him there, too many whores and pimps, and went back to his old trade of breeding and dealing in horses. To complete his reformation, he booked his journey to Mecca and accomplished the holy pilgrimage which made him a hajji – 'not from that money I made in India, believe you me,' he assured the Muslim travel agent who chuckled with a sceptical smile as to the halal character of his cash.

But on this particular day, with the morning sun preparing to make the ceramic tiles of the *haush* dazzling to the eyes, Abu Mamduh had different business to attend to. His jaws tightened as he bit on his lower lip and listened to the women protesting and pleading in different tones and from diverse angles of appeal. Mindful that members of the female sex always get what they want in the end by the simple tactic of repetition, Aunt Wafiah rephrased the words of the Koran: 'Repent ye and ye receive forgiveness. That is what the Almighty God tells you, Abu Mamduh, my dear.'

By way of supporting her older sister and expressing general solidarity with feminism, Aunt Salima joined in the hubbub. 'To be sure, girls in their teens develop all sorts of mysterious symptoms and quirks. When I was that age, I could never have a bath with my pants off.'

Her ancient, stooping mother sat silently, her drooping lips trembling uncontrollably. She nodded her head in approval, releasing a stream of saliva from the side of her mouth which she hastily wiped with the edge of her *hijab*.

It was time for one more aunt, dressed in silk, to chip in, but her ill-fitting, upper denture slipped, preventing her from finishing her sentence: 'I believe the girl should . . . ' With her tattooed hand she removed the loose denture, dried it with her sleeve and put it back in position. 'I was going to say . . . ' The pink and white plate fell again.

'Um Halim,' blurted out the woman sitting opposite, 'this bloody new denture of yours is no bloody good. I told you many times not to go to Dr Hussein al-Agha, the Persian dentist at the end of the bridge. Go to the Armenian, Dr Garibian. It would cost you two more dinars but you would get a reliable set.'

'You can never trust a Persian with anything,' agreed Aunt Malika as she produced her own denture. 'Look! Perfect fitting! The work of the Armenian dentist. I always say that when you need something done, go to an Armenian. From shoe repair to teeth repair, you can find no one better than an Armenian.'

'True. As the saying goes, one Jew equals ten Persians, but one Armenian equals ten Jews.' The women found the subject of teeth and dentistry most interesting and indulged in it wholeheartedly. In the meantime, the subject of the wretched girl was com-pletely brushed aside. That discussion exhausted, they turned to politics and the subject of Palestine and the British. 'I always say that wherever there is trouble it is Abu Naji behind it. As is well known, no fish in water turns its tail without the same Abu Naji moving it.' Abu Naji was and is the nickname which the Iraqis gave to Britain and the British. It was a poetic borrowing from a Jewish businessman, Abu Naji, through whom Miss Gertrude Bell, the British secretary of the Mandate administration, used to filter the plans of the British Government to the local population. The conversation drifted from one subject to the other like the bloated corpses of lambs and goats carried here and there by the flooding rivers of the angry Tigris and the rebellious Euphrates with all their tributaries. Eventually, the same Aunt Wafia, who seemed the most concerned about the fate of the young fallen girl, restarted the case for the defence.

'My dear Abu Mamduh, may God keep you in good health and give you a long life, let us go back to the Shari'a. What does it say? The sin of a woman must be proved by four good witnesses seeing the act of copulation with their own eyes, seeing the rod in the kohl pot, as the Prophet Muhammad, peace be upon him, stipulated. 'Where are these four witnesses?'

'Yes. And what's more she is an unmarried woman. What does the Holy Koran say? It says whip her a hundred strokes. No killing in the Koran, Haj Abu Mamduh.'

This learned disputation was interrupted by Um

Mamduh, who came out of the kitchen carrying a copper tray with eight small *istikans* of tea almost as black as creosote which she offered to the guests. Um Mamduh, or Aisha bint Abdul Razzaq, to give her her full maiden name, was a round woman with a slumped figure, inflated belly and an angular face. She wore no *hijab*. She was in her own house and no strangers were around to see her. She must have preceded the mini-skirt fashion by some two decades or more for the hem of her dress fell well above her fat, bulky knees. The two cats followed the lady with their bright eyes and purred in approval as she went back to the dim kitchen to fetch a silver basket full of *ka'ak*, a local type of long and thick biscuit covered with sesame. With tea and biscuits being served and savoured, to the sound of the clattering of teaspoons, the subject and fate of Samira was once more shelved – until another old aunt, who had finished drinking her tea and placed the gold-decorated *istikan* back on the copper tray in front of her, composed herself and restarted the argument.

Cousin Sadiqa presented what seemed to her a practical solution. 'Why not take Samira to Basra to live with her aunts in the guise of a serving maid until everything is revealed. If she turns out to be pregnant, a young man called for military service might be induced to marry her and secure his exemption from the army for disgracing the honour of the valiant Iraqi armed forces by marrying a common whore.'

All the women held their breath as well as their tongues. Even the hubble-bubble in front of Haj Nufal stopped gurgling. The solemn silence of the grave had to be broken by a man. The hajji breathed out a cloud of cool tobacco smoke and replenished his lungs with a fresh intake of clean air. Raising his balding head towards the heavens above, he snapped, 'Mamduh! Ya Mamduh, where are you?'

A young voice answered his call, 'Yes, dad, coming. Waiting for Ahmad.'

Abu Mamduh turned to his female folk to give them his answer. 'There is no need to worry. If she is innocent, no one is going to touch her. If not and if she has disgraced our name by becoming a plaything for some lecherous young man, she will deserve what she gets.'

Failing to dissuade their kinsman, the women tried another route. Attack is the best form of defence. 'But who is to blame in all this wretched business?' snorted the shrewd Malika. 'It was all your fault. This is an idea you picked up from your Jewish friends in Bombay – to send your daughter to school. What do girls learn from school? Nothing but dis-obedience and fornication.'

'Blasphemies and immorality.'

'They tell them monkeys created man and not the Almighty Allah. I could understand it if they said it was man who created the monkeys. But this fellow Tarwin tells them it was the monkeys who made man.'

15

'I have seen these schoolgirls bouncing about in the playing field in shorts no bigger than a pigeon's tail, laughing and shouting.'

'When you hear a girl laughing loudly, she is half way to losing her virginity.'

'Anyway, who is responsible?' cousin Malika resumed her attack. 'It is her father who sent her to this rowdy school in al-Risafah. They are all Kurds and Turks there who don't know what is right and what is wrong. Half of the women there are prostitutes.'

'Why didn't he send her to the Laura Kadoorie Jewish School? He is always with the Jews.'

'Ya, they know how to educate their girls.'

Silence was resumed but was soon interrupted by the sound of footsteps coming down the tiled stairs. Two young men, in outdoor clothing, of equal height and build and with identical moustaches, appeared in the *haush*. Although similar in appearance, both with jet-black curly hair and knotted eyebrows, they differed in their general demeanour. One, obviously the elder, walked with determination and ease; his younger brother, Ahmad, had the look of a worried student unprepared for his finals. He fidgeted and stumbled once or twice in the few steps which took him from the stairs to where his father sat. They both wore gabardine raincoats, slightly out of season for that time of year in central Iraq. Ahmad had both hands in the large pockets of his raincoat and looked as if he was digging for something in them. Mamduh had both hands free but his coat seemed uncomfortable on his sturdy figure and even askew, with one side pulling at the other. The younger son walked at the heels of his elder brother and stood hesitantly behind him, not for any particular respect for the older, but because of an inner turmoil in his heart which expressed itself in uncontrollable nodding and scratching.

Having removed the brass end of the hubble-bubble pipe from his mouth and wiped his curling lips, the father addressed his elder son, 'Where is your sister?'

'She is getting ready, dad.'

'Have you talked to her? It is her last chance. Have you asked her?'

'We did, dad. We did. But she wouldn't answer. She wouldn't talk. She just sobs and cries.'

'You have your weapons with you? Show me.'

The two young men put their hands in their coat pockets and produced two identical pistols, small and new looking. The women gasped and murmured. Sadiqa turned her face away and Sumayya and Salima, looking small and frightened, uttered some brief incantation against the devil. Wafiah tried again to appeal to Haj Nufal, but he silenced her with an angry gesture of his hand, pointing the brass end of the pipe at her face like a weapon.

'Are they properly loaded?'

'Yes, dad. I hope we won't need to use them.'

'So do I.'

Mamduh pressed a catch and unloaded his gun.

Five bullets in all, shining new. He put them back and closed the gun. Ahmad followed suit with trembling hands. All the while the women looked nervous, struck with fear and foreboding, gesticulating, murmuring and hissing like injured animals. 'Allah, save us from the accursed devil. There is no power or device except those of Allah. Messenger of God, help us, lead us, have mercy on us . . . Oh, Abu Mamduh, have mercy, curse the devil. Listen to us . . . '

'Why are you standing here in front of me like the trunk of a dead palm tree? Go and fetch your sister.'

'Ahmad, go and hurry her up. The surgery may soon close.' Mamduh echoed his father's order. Ahmad put his revolver in his pocket again and went upstairs with bowed head and unsure feet, looking back at his father once or twice. In less than a minute, a thin, black cloud appeared at the top of the staircase. Slowly it descended into the *haush*, following the track of the bewildered Ahmad. Samira was wrapped in a long black cloak, an *abaya*, covering her entire figure from head to foot, but as she moved into the passageway leading to the front door and the outside world, she halted for a second, lifted her *burqu'*, the traditional thin veil, and cast a brief look at the throng gathered in the *iwan*. Her face was the colour of a brown organic egg. The eyes, although downcast and almost closed, flickered brightly through long dark eyelashes. The knotted eyebrows attested to her relationship to her two older brothers. She really was their sister, as people often remarked, much to her pleasurable pride. She was, however much smaller in her physique and slightly shorter, some five feet or so, but quite tall among the women of her race and country. She opened her parched lips, adorned on the right and below with two beauty spots of blue tattoo, trembling and twisting, to murmur a few words in the way of a painful farewell. They were hardly audible but the icy silence made them sound like an *izzan* from a minaret.

'God be with you.'

The old man closed his eyes but could not prevent a teardrop from trickling down his cheek, warm and salty. He really loved his daughter.

'There is no power or device except that of Allah.'

'Whatever is written, so it shall pass.'

The silence resumed until broken by the sound of the front door closing behind the two brothers, followed by their hapless sister. They negotiated the winding narrow lanes from al-Mishahdah through Suq al-Jadid and to the *sikka*, the tramway. The lanes were wet with the dirty soapy water poured out by the dwellers. There was no pavement and the three had to hug the central open sewer, dodging from side to side. When they arrived at the *sikka* to catch the *garry*, the double-deck tram drawn by a couple of emaciated and exhausted horses, they found the unhappy beasts lying on the track, unable to stand or indeed make any move, their parched mouths wide open, their white teeth sticking out and their eyes rolling. Their protruding ribs sank and rose with rhythmic spurts as they lay huffing and puffing. 'Bring them water. Hurry up for the love of God,' shouted someone in Hamdun's coffee house, near by. The heavy tram was packed with people, some hundred passengers or more, many of them hanging on to the windows outside the tram, swearing and shouting. It was getting late in the day and Mamduh was forced to hire a *rabal*, a horse-drawn carriage.

'Damnation! Whenever you want to do some serious business affecting your honour, Satan, curse be upon him, comes in between and frustrates your mission.'

'Damn it all!' echoed his younger brother.

The two brothers sat on the high seat and Samira took her place in front of them on the lower un-upholstered seat, completely wrapped in black, just like a giant piece of charcoal resting on a pair of pale-green sandals.

'Akh! Deeee . . . ' shouted the coachman as he gave his two coffee-coloured horses a high-whistling lash from his long whip. The carriage pulled away, helter-skelter, jingling noisily, with the three young people swaying and shaking on their bumpy way to the unknown.

'God forgive us all,' whimpered the living creature inside the piece of charcoal with a sigh.

🦋 2 🦋

No Choice

Baghdad's main thoroughfare, Rashid Street, joined up with King Ghazi Street and Sadun Street at the King Faisal II Square, east of the old city, flanked on one side by a silent Christian convent with a girls' secondary school attached to it, run by nuns for the adolescent daughters of the rich, the leading military commanders and the top bureaucrats of the country, and on the other side, only a little distance farther away, by a loud mosque, blasting its call to prayer five times a day from its giant loudspeakers. This summons was invariably followed by the chiming of the Armenian Church's bells. The phenomenon, part of the traditional Muslim tolerance of other faiths, inspired the great eleventh-century poet and philosopher al-Ma'arri to say:

> In Lattakia, there is a conflict
> Between Jesus and Muhammad,
> The one rings with his bells, the other shouts
> from his minaret,
> Each calling for his religion.
> Oh, my muse, would that I knew,
> Which of them is true!

Moses kept out of it and the synagogue, a few hundred metres away, maintained its silence, for Judaism is something to be whispered between a Jew and a Jew only.

Rashid Street ran parallel to the Tigris River which split the city into two unequal sides in perpetual conflict. The southern side, al-Karkh, was the original site of the Abbasid circular city facing the desert and Arabia. It was built by the Khalif Abu Ja'far al-Mansur sometime during the eighth century. The north-eastern side, al-Risafah, looked towards Iran, central Asia and Byzantium. The physical division produced an anthropological distribution, with mainly Sunni Arabs living in al-Karkh and a cosmopolitan conglomeration of Kurds, Uzbekistanis, Turks, Jews, Christians and Muslims of all denominations living side by side and quite comfortably in al-Risafah.

Sadun Street, which stretched at the east end of al-Risafah, was lined on both sides by cafés, restaurants, bookshops, grocers, pharmacies, cinemas and cabarets. As you walked along the broken pavement beside the sewer, you would encounter different smells every few metres, starting with that of lamb kebab, grilled liver and boiled chick peas and ending with the aroma of arak, the national drink, and the pharmaceutical concoctions breathing out from the chemists' shops. Here and there you would find the inevitable beggar, male or female, young or old, and sellers of sherbet, liquid yoghurt, iced water and salted nuts. Vendors of lottery tickets drowned out, with their loud promises, the street cries of the wandering sellers of boiled turnips, a staple food consumed abundantly in winter as a sure remedy for coughs and colds.

All this was to be seen and heard at ground level; above, on the first and second floors, were the offices of lawyers, businessmen and fortune tellers and the various clinics of medical practitioners, among whom was Dr Abdul Salam Sassoon, a Jewish gynae-cologist trained at University College Hospital in London. He first studied medicine at Baghdad's prestigious Faculty of Medicine which was run by an English doctor, Dr Anderson. Sassoon studied with his schoolmate, George Malik, a Christian from the little Chaldian town of Talkaif in the province of Nineveh, just a few miles north of Mosul. Their interest in music had brought them together. Both attended the Institute of Fine Arts opposite the Royal Court in the Najib Pasha district. Young George Malik studied Western music and played the violin, while Sassoon studied Eastern music and played the oud. The difference in orientation and religion, however, had not prevented them from developing a close friendship. They often drank arak together at one of the cheaper pubs in Battaween and went out to Kallachia, the great, red-light district of the city. In more sober days, they sat at George's flat and spent their time artistically, with George playing Mozart, Beethoven and Vivaldi, and Sassoon playing the oud compositions of Professor Sharif Muhi Aldean and Arabic folklore songs associated with the renowned Jewish singer Salima Murad. Endowed with a reasonable voice, Sassoon often sang some of her popular songs, as any Iraqi might do, as well as the standard Egyptian songs of Muhammad Abd al-Wahhab and Farid al-Atrash. When in a good mood, he would try to render some of the classic *maqam* songs of Muhammad al-Qubbanchi.

Upon graduation from school, they joined the Faculty of Medicine of the Royal Hospital at Bab al-Mu'addam. The clever boys and girls of the Jewish and Christian communities of Iraq found medicine a good field of professional life which spared them any involvement with the Muslim majority and the running of the country's affairs. Rather than being supplicants of the domineering Muslims, with medicine they made the Muslims, ever preoccupied with their health, dependent on them. It was always customary for Jews and Christians in the Arab world to choose careers which gave them independence. Medicine, they found, was a prestigious career and well paid at that.

As it happened, young George and young Abdul Salam did not differ in their musical tastes alone, they also differed in their attitude towards and understanding of medicine. George thought that, in

the Middle East, the shortest route to the people's
pockets was through their stomachs, for nothing
mattered to them more than eating and they were
always eating the wrong things at the wrong time
since they often had the wrong eating habits. Abdul
Salam Sassoon differed from his friend on this
matter. True, he thought that one of the two items
which preoccupied the minds of the people in the
Middle East was food, but sex had, unquestionably,
the upper hand, so to speak. He repeatedly argued
with his friend that their real interest was not in
their stomachs, but in their penises. This is, undoubtedly, he thought, the shortest route to their
pockets. They will give anything for a good woman's
vagina and a bigger penis. The result was that Dr
George Malik specialised in the digestive tract while
Abdul Salam Sassoon went on to become a gynaecologist. As the top consultant in his field, all the
quality sexual organs of the leading ladies of Iraqi
society were quite familiar to him. Dr Abdul Salam
Sassoon knew all about their sexual curricula vitae
and their biological histories, as he was the trusted
Jew who spent most of his time stitching up their
broken hymens at twenty dinars a time and keeping
his mouth shut to everyone's satisfaction.

Medicine and music were not his only interests.
Like most young Jews of his generation, he dabbled
in the country's left-wing politics and helped in the
translation of many classic Marxist texts into Arabic.

It was part of his sensitive nature and his concern for the orphaned and the deprived. Many times he refused to take fees from a poor woman worn out by repeated pregnancies and miscarriages. Sometimes, he even paid for his patients' prescriptions himself. He was tall and slim, and made to look even more so by his balding head and thick black moustache. It was always perplexing to see him putting on his thick glasses whenever he talked to his patients and taking them off whenever he read or wrote their prescriptions. Five years in England did not rid him of the Baghdadi habit of always touching his balls and readjusting the position of his penis whenever he walked, nor of fondling his moustache whenever he had nothing better to do or to say. It was just that he could not keep his hands still, another trait of Mediterranean peoples. Yet, in the case of Dr Abdul Salam it was likely that this mannerism was also an outward sign of inward turmoil and anxiety. Frequently, he relied on his thick charcoal-black eyebrows and deeply lined forehead to make sure of delivering whatever message or expression he wanted to communicate to his visitors.

With the substantial money he made in his Rashid Street surgery, just next to al-Watani cinema, he moved to a more spacious clinic of his own in Sadun Street, occupying the entire first floor of a modern block. In addition to the large reception area, furnished with European-style (Louis-Quatorze) seating, there was his consulting-room, a secretarial office and a little operating and delivery theatre, with all the essential equipment for a practising gynaecologist. In contrast to this little theatre, the consulting-room was somewhat *outré* for a medical man, as one wall contained oil paintings by Iraq's most notable artists, such as Faik Hassan and Jawad Salim. On the opposite wall, facing the east, Dr Abdul Salam Sassoon had hung two old – probably antique – musical stringed instruments. The shelves behind him were loaded with books on literature and Marxist theory and the history of the working class rather than reference books on gynaecology or the physiology of the female body.

This most unusual clinic was above two shops, one of which was a pharmacy, whose owner maintained an excellent relationship with the doctor above and used to send him a continuous stream of customers. 'If you search the whole country from Mosul to Basra, you will never find a doctor as good as Dr Sassoon,' Mufid, the chemist, used to say to his callers. Abdul Aziz, the butcher, on the other hand, who kept the other shop, had a different answer for anyone asking him about the doctor. 'Oh, he moved away a long time ago. Sorry, I don't know where he has gone.' This unkind misinformation was the butcher's response to the doctor's frequent directive to his patients: 'Don't eat meat.' No love was lost between the two kinds of butcher. The meat trader often chided the doctor's customers by bringing in religion. 'Have you no shame? How can you allow a Jew to look at your wife's body, to poke his fingers into her private parts? Isn't there a Muslim doctor to do that for you?'

There were no hours fixed for the practice so as the last patient, a woman with fertility problems, finished her examination and departed with her husband, Dr Sassoon prepared to pack up his things and leave for home. Just as he was about to turn off the lights, his secretary-nurse came in, looking rather bothered and annoyed. 'Dr Sassoon, two odd-looking men want to see you.'

'Did you say two men?'

'Yes, doctor. Both have their faces wrapped up in *keffiyehs* of red-and-white check.'

'Never mind the colours. Two of them, you say?'

'Yes, doctor. They want to see you urgently.'

'Strange! Didn't you tell them that this is a gynae-cology clinic? They have probably made a mistake. Possibly they don't know what gynaecology is.'

'I told them so. They know. They are quite educated, doctor, probably poets.'

Dr Sassoon recalled that in the Gulf area men did indeed marry men. But this was Iraq and that was no business for a gynaecologist. A doctor of venereal disease, yes, but surely no gynaecologist's province.

'There is a woman with them. I presume she is a

woman for she is all wrapped up in black. They wouldn't let me see her face.'

'Well, bring the woman in.'

The secretary-nurse went out but returned in less than a minute without anyone.

'Well! The men say they want to see you themselves without the woman. I don't like the sound of it. It seems suspicious.'

'Well, bring the men in then.'

The baffled nurse went out and came back with the two of them. Their bizarre appearance matched their bizarre visit. Large sunglasses, with lenses the size of orange leaves, covered half their faces, making them look like some weird detectives in an old film. Exactly as the nurse had described, their mystery was enhanced by the fact that they wore *keffiyehs* of red-and-white check, quite unusual for educated gentlemen in European suits and Saxone shoes. Just as the consultant was baffled by their strange appearance, so were they baffled by the paintings and musical instruments hanging on the walls. Indeed the older of the two was prompted to put this understandable question: 'Are you Dr Abdul Salam Sassoon and is this his clinic?' He turned his head to examine the strange contents of the surgery.

'Yes, that is right. What can I do for you?'

'So you are, indeed, Dr Sassoon, the gynaecologist.'

'The doctor gynaecologist,' repeated the younger man, parrot like.

This brief interrogation was followed by a pause of embarrassed silence until the doctor was forced to repeat his question: 'What can I do for you, my friends? I take it that you are here for a medical enquiry. Anything wrong with you?'

'No,' said the older.

'No,' echoed the younger.

'It is something concerning our sister.'

'The woman sitting in the waiting-room? Why don't you bring her in?'

'We suspect that she is pregnant. Some wicked son-of-a-bitch played around with her.'

'I understand.'

'No, you don't. We want you to examine her properly and tell us.'

'That is easy.'

'No, it isn't.'

'No, it isn't,' repeated the younger man looking at his companion.

'We want you to examine her and tell us the truth of the matter. If she is really pregnant, we want you to cut her open and remove the baby. Bring it to us to see it and make sure of what you tell us. Once that is done, God forbid, we want you to kill her and dispose of her body in your own professional way. You are head of the gynaecological department, a professional consultant, and have the means of getting rid of anybody's corpse. Issue it with a death certificate, identifying it as one of an unknown prostitute who came to you because of a miscarriage or for an abortion and died under your hands. We want no trace left of her real identity. We are a respectable family. We'll see to the rest.'

'Yes, respectable family – very,' reiterated the younger man, getting more and more nervous, but certainly no more nervous than the doctor, who was by now visibly fidgeting and trembling. Involuntarily, he put his hand on the telephone only to withdraw it with alacrity and put it in his pocket. He wanted to say something and opened his mouth but he shut it again without saying anything or producing any sound other than that of the clenching of teeth. The two visitors exchanged anxious looks and then turned towards him earnestly.

'To do this job you will receive eight hundred dinars from us. I have the money with me,' said the older brother, pointing to the wallet in his pocket.

'What if I find that she is still a virgin and not pregnant?'

'You will then receive twenty dinars only. But listen carefully. If you deceive us and the girl's stomach shows signs of growing bigger, we'll come back and empty this gun into your head.' The man put his hand in his pocket and produced his pistol, thus prompting his brother to do the same. 'We'll follow you to the ends of the earth.'

'Listen, my friends. Why are you coming to me? There are many other doctors who can do this examination. Why do you come to a Jewish doctor?'

'We can trust you. You won't talk. Jews don't talk.'

Dr Sassoon suggested many constructive alternatives in an attempt to persuade these unwelcome clients to spare him the horrors of this impending tragedy. Try to get her lover to marry her. Abort the baby, if there was one, and make good the damage. Send her abroad to study something or other. Pay some needy person to marry her. Wait for her to complete her nine months and have the baby adopted or given away to the Child Protection Charity. Yet none of these solutions was acceptable to them. The girl had committed a cardinal sin and would have to pay for it with her life. It is the logic of a poor nation and a practical formula, cruel as it is, for population control. Women must not be allowed promiscuously to produce more mouths to feed in a land threatened with famine. Each female is born equipped with a population-control key in the form of a hymen. It can only be turned to open by the fittest candidate, the rich suitor who can afford to pay the dowry and to feed the offspring. The men of God recognized these facts and imposed their rationale by laying down strict rules for the game and function of procreation. The rest of the community obeyed and so did the rest of the Haj Nufal family.

Mamduh and Ahmad produced their guns for the second time and pointed them at the unfortunate Dr Sassoon. Either do what you are told to do or prepare your ears for bangs from both the loaded pistols.

No way could his decision be postponed. The family
honour is at stake and the odds are loaded against
the Jew.

'Bring her in then.'

'No, not until your nurse goes. This is a very confidential business.'

Dr Sassoon was clearly nonplussed by this request.
However, he found he was quite curious about the
whole thing and his curiosity took over and prompted
him to ring the nurse and send her away, which
pleased her as it would any other medical staff.
Mamduh indicated to his brother to put his gun back
in his pocket and fetch his sister. Having introduced
her to Dr Sassoon and asked her to take off her *abaya*
and obey the doctor's instructions, they left the
surgery and went out to endure the tortuous minutes
of waiting, neither daring to say a word to each other.
The waiting-room's old clock ticked away, dispersing
the remaining daylight from the establishment.
Mamduh got up, drew the curtains neatly and put on
the light. 'La ilaha illa Allah,' he whispered to himself
before sitting down again.

'Taking a long time,' sighed young Ahmed to give
vent to his tightened chest while randomly tapping
his heels on the floor. He finally lifted his bottom
from the chair and walked around the room aim-
lessly, looking at the dusty pictures and framed
medical diplomas hanging on the walls.

'Sit down! Sit down! What is the matter with you?'

asked Mamduh. He received no answer to his sensible question, but he managed to make his brother sink again into his seat.

'What will be, will be.'

Just when Mamduh was about to pick up the daily newspaper, *al-Bilad*, the door opened and they caught the sound of a woman's sob before Dr Abdul Salam Sassoon closed it gently behind him. His look of unalloyed despondency and doom was squarely matched on the faces of the two young men in front of him. After a couple of dry coughs and a nervous pull at his trousers, he opened his mouth, closed it, and opened it again with another cough.

'I am sorry. I don't have good news for you. The girl is pregnant.'

'The evidence! We want to see the evidence.'

'Yes, we want the evidence,' echoed Ahmad, the words, dry as small pieces of pitta bread, minced and broken at almost every syllable.

The doctor swallowed and wore a beseeching look. 'My friends, do you really want me to go through with all that? You can trust my word. I can show you the signs. Just leave her here for another day. Perhaps you will change your mind. Consult your father. She says she is only sixteen. A very young thing.'

'We must obey our father's instructions. If she is with child, she must not leave this surgery alive.'

'Please take her to another doctor, a Muslim

doctor. I need an anaesthetist. I need the help of a nurse. My nurse, Victoria, is gone. Don't you understand?'

Mamduh put his hand in his pocket where he had the gun, loaded and cocked. Ahmad followed suit. Dr Abdul Salam Sassoon understood the gesture and the implication. 'No, she won't be taken to another doctor. You just do what we are telling you. There are ten bullets in our guns. You will share them equally with her. Five for you, five for her. We want to see the evidence.'

Mamduh walked determinedly to the outer door and locked it on the inside, giving the key to his brother for safekeeping. His next move was to pull out the telephone cable thus disconnecting the receiver. In despair, Dr Abdul Salam Sassoon threw his arms in the air, shook his head repeatedly and gasped resignedly, 'Oh, God.' Still facing the unwelcome callers, he walked back to his examination room with hesitant backward steps. Once he was out of sight, the two brothers took their hands out of their pockets and slumped on the empty sofa, their lips trembling with words recited under his breath. It was time for prayers, shared in silence and with eyes not raised up to heaven but downcast to the floor.

The clock struck eight. No sign of the doctor yet. 'Why can't they shut up?' protested one of the boys as the cries of the street peddlers and ice-cream sellers were becoming unbearable. The record player of the coffee house opposite was blaring out the voice of Afifa Iskander singing:

> '*Daqiqa,*
> *Ismah li min fadhlak daqiqa,*
> *Alshan aqullak bilhaqiqa.*

'One minute,
Please give me one minute,
One minute to tell you the truth.'

The song was soon mixed up with the barking of a pack of stray dogs fighting over something thrown out to them from the nearby restaurant.

'Blast! This is all we need to hear now. Dogs fighting over a bitch.'

'Why can't someone shoot her and put a stop to their barking.'

Ahmad took out his pistol and emptied its magazine into his hand. He examined the bullets, shaking them by his ear, wiped them with his shirt sleeve to shine them and put them back where they belonged. At this moment, the door of the examination room opened and Dr Abdul Salam Sassoon emerged with a bundle of newspaper. He looked perturbed and shaky in his operating gown and gloves, with none of the composure one normally expects in a surgeon. The two men got up with no less perturbation as they received the soiled paper. Both stretched their necks to look inside it with eyes opened as wide as their sinews would allow.

'This is it. This is what you wanted to see,' stammered the shaken doctor.

'Ahmad, can you see any resemblance? Any trace of Hassun in it?'

'I can't tell. But, surely it must have been him, who else could it have been? The bastard was always chasing her wherever she went,' answered the fear-stricken young Ahmad, looking like one who is about to throw up as Mamduh extended one of his fingers to touch the foetus.

'It is still warm.' He covered up the little thing with the newspaper and handed it back to Dr Sassoon. 'Is she conscious? Does she know? I mean – the fruit of her wicked sin?'

'No, she is still asleep.'

'Well, she won't wake up this time,' muttered the elder brother through his teeth. Then, more hesitatingly, 'Can we have a last look at our sister?'

'No, I don't advise it. It will haunt you to the end of your life.'

'Please.'

Dr Sassoon scratched his chin and his head as he thought for a moment before replying with reluctance: 'Well, if you insist. But it will have to be a very brief look. Give me a minute first.'

Dr Sassoon went back into the little theatre and covered the girl entirely, allowing only her face to be seen. She lay unconscious, her mouth wide open but her eyes closed, fringed with long black eyelashes.

The curls of her dark hair fell against the white sheet as in a picture. Her toes, with their red-painted nails, peeped out from beneath the sheet, turned up as if in supplication to the great one above. Young Ahmad could not suppress his feelings and burst into tears like an adolescent girl at an Imam Hussein Lamentation.

The doctor led them out. 'This is enough.'

For Mamduh his mission was accomplished, except for one thing. He wiped his hand with his handkerchief and produced his wallet. 'We said eight hundred dinars.'

'No, please. I can't accept money for this work.'

'Why not? You still have to see to the final details and dispose of her body. It will cost you something, doctor.'

'I'll pay for that myself. Just go and keep quiet about it. It is a grave responsibility. No one should know.'

'That is what we are asking of you. The Hanifi is a very respectable family. Nothing like this has ever happened to us before. No one must hear of it. She brought disgrace upon all of us with her sin. My poor father!'

'He will get over it.'

'Are you sure you won't accept any fee. Any money? We feel guilty.'

'Very sure,' said Dr Sassoon, as he went on nodding his head pensively.

The two unwelcome callers put out their arms to shake hands. He had to take off his rubber gloves and meet, reluctantly, this disagreeable gesture before retrieving the key from Ahmad and leading them to the door. He listened to their footsteps as they went down the stairs and into the bustle of Sadun Street. Afifa Iskander was repeating her song:

> 'One minute,
> Please give me one minute,
> One minute to tell you the truth.'

3

Encounter

Poor Nurse Victoria had to make excuses for the doctor's unexpected disappearance and endure the wrath of the impatient patients who could not understand that a doctor might also fall sick and need days off work like anyone else. In the absence, in Iraq, of any arrangement to cancel appointments or warn the patients, Dr Sassoon's customers had to travel all the way from Samarra or Karbala, in some cases on mules for part of the distance, only to find the surgery closed and the doctor unavailable. Victoria's Christian faith did not help her either, as the women-folk attributed their disappointment and her negative words to her anti-Muslim crusader spirit, especially when she could not tell them when the good doctor would be back. 'There we are, fallen between a Jew and a Christian,' one woman protested angrily. 'They don't care if I lose my baby. For them, it will be one Muslim fewer.'

For almost a week after his unhappy encounter with the Hanifi boys, Dr Abdul Salam Sassoon did not attend his clinic. He was neither in the hospital nor at home, which left his wife with no option but to inform the police, who did nothing other than put it on record. They shrugged their shoulders and probably thought that the doctor had gone away with one of his nice-looking patients for a love adventure. Others thought that it was a case of one fewer Jew.

At the end of the week, on the Sabbath as it happened, he reappeared at his clinic, much to the relief of his nurse, to say nothing of his patients, pregnant or still trying. 'Haven't I told you? The doctor was ill. Don't you understand? Male doctors may not get pregnant but they do fall ill, like you,' shouted Nurse Victoria Hanna to the crowded waiting-room.

'Thanks be to Allah. May he give him a long and healthy life.'

Invented as it was, Victoria's guess was not altogether untrue. Abdul Salam Sassoon was indeed unwell and could not eat or sleep for many days. He was forced, in the end, to take some medication and vitamins, which was the medical fashion in the Middle East. Even within this very brief period, he seemed to have lost weight and looked pale and languid. His eyes were shining but were watery and restless. His nurse noticed that he had acquired quite a few new habits and mannerisms, like biting his pen, scratching his head, pursing his lips and rubbing his eyes. His appearance was untidy and neglected. He wore his white shirt but forgot to put on his tie or button up his shirt cuffs. Altogether, there was a marked change in his demeamour and mood, which lacked its usual gaiety and humour. He had lost much of his ability to concentrate.

Victoria Hanna had to repeat most of what she said and still failed to get the expected response.

'Did you hear what I've just said, doctor? A strange young man came every day, sometimes twice a day, enquiring after you. He seemed so anxious to see you. He looked rough and troubled in mind. I am sure he will be coming again. He wouldn't give me his name though, or explain what he wanted from you.'

'Never mind that. Probably he wants some contraception to enable him to sleep with his girlfriend. That is when they become so anxious. They want to sleep with a girl without a condom and yet they are afraid of making her pregnant. The same old story. You have the set reply. Give it to him.'

'I gave it to him. I told him there is no contraceptive here. But he said he wasn't coming for that.'

The nurse was quite right in saying that the young man would soon come again. For no sooner had she finished her conversation with her employer than she heard the bell ringing. She opened the door and there was the same young man in front of her, that rough-looking young man, troubled in his mind.

'Dr Abdul Salam Sassoon is back now in his clinic. I saw him going up the stairs. I have been watching the clinic all day.'

'Indeed!'

'Sister, it is very serious. I must see him immediately.'

Nurse Victoria led him into the consulting-room and introduced him to Dr Abdul Salam. Brief as it was, the nurse's description of him was apt and correct. The young man looked rough indeed and troubled. His face had not seen a razor blade for a number of days and his hazel eyes looked wild and worried, and slightly bloodshot. He was broad-shouldered, tall and slim. His face had the complexion of a white chocolate bar. Whenever he spoke, he felt that his words were inadequate and needed some physical emphasis, which was generously given by his frequent hand gestures and the raising of his eyebrows. Not only that, but even his slick tongue seemed to polish his words by licking his lips at every syllable. Lush curls of dark brown hair, the colour of a wet oak barrel, were in disarray, covering almost all his forehead and displaying some remnants of Brylcreem, which was fashionable among the younger generation during the forties and fifties of the twentieth century. His clothes had seen better days, yet not too far in the past. So had his designer shoes, now very much down-at-heel in two shades of plain leather and suede. It was one of those rare days in Baghdad when it rained abundantly, causing the young man's complete attire to look brighter and richer in colour. He wiped his shoes as he entered Dr Abdul Salam Sassoon's consulting-room, indicating some civilized manners and good breeding which contrasted with his present state of slovenliness.

'I understand that my nurse has told you that we provide no contraception here. In fact, my young man, there is no real contraception other than rubber condoms which you can buy from the chemist downstairs at a hundred fils per packet of three. But it seems this is not what you are after.'

'Certainly not. I wish I had used them. By God, I wish I had!'

'What is it then? If you want me to stitch up the broken hymen of some woman you know, then I advise you straight away to look for some other doctor. We don't do that here – neither I nor my nurse. You know, I am a professor at the Faculty of Medicine.'

'No, doctor, no. I know that. I am not looking for an abortion job either. I am here to enquire about something else. I have reason to believe that you examined a certain young lady a few days ago.'

'I examine young and old ladies all the time. That is what I do.'

'A young lady by the name of Samira. She was brought to you to establish whether she was pregnant.'

Dr Sassoon adjusted his glasses and fixed his visitor with a piercing look. 'Look here, young man, you must know that we medical people are under oath not to reveal any information concerning our patients. Our work is strictly confidential. Whether it was Samira, Sahira or Fadhila, don't come here and ask me about her. Please, that is enough and I ask you to leave this room without any more fuss.'

The young man suddenly broke down, threw himself on the empty seat and started sobbing. Dr Sassoon rushed to him, patted him on the head and tried to console him. The doctor seemed on the verge of tears himself. He took his visitor to the examination couch and sat beside him, his arm round his shoulders, shaking him gently.

'Thank you, Dr Abdul Salam,' the youth sobbed, 'The truth is that I am Samira's lover. The child she is carrying is my child. She has disappeared completely since she was brought to you to examine her. Her parents don't talk about her. I must know. Has she been murdered? Is she still alive? If so, I must look for her.'

'What is your name, my boy?'

'Hassun. Hassun Abd al-Ali.'

'Now listen to me, Hassun. I examined your girlfriend, as you said, and found her to be about three months pregnant. I had to tell her brothers the truth. There was no way for me to tell them otherwise. I wish that I could have, but they threatened to kill me. You are a Muslim, Hassun, and you know how sensitive your people are in these matters. They are quite prepared to sacrifice anything, to lose anything, even their own country, but not the honour of their womenfolk. I had to tell them the facts of the situation. They are Muslims and I am a Jew.'

Hassun had stopped sobbing. He took a handkerchief proffered by Dr Sassoon and wiped his eyes, nose and cheeks. 'Thank you, doctor.' Steadying himself, he faced his interlocutor once more with an appealing look verging on the pathetic. He stretched out his hands in supplication. 'Please, doctor, help me. What happened to Samira? You must know, doctor, what happened to her?'

'How should I know? A doctor's job finishes with his diagnosis and treatment. It is none of his business to poke into a patient's affairs and private life – what they do or don't do.'

'Is she still alive?'

'Ask her parents. She is their daughter and they should know.'

The young lover, now in a state of despair, lost all hope of soliciting any more information from Abdul Salam Sassoon. 'Anyway, doctor, thank you for seeing me. Thank you for giving me so much of your time. I am sorry, doctor, I have no money to pay for this visit.'

'I wouldn't take it,' said the doctor with a jovial smile. 'But take my advice. Don't waste your time and wreck your health and your future. You are still a young man. You will soon forget her. Meet another girl and start a new love affair – a second, a third, a fourth one. These things happen to young people all the time. Just forget all about her.'

'Thank you, doctor.'

In the course of their conversation, Dr Abdul

Salam Sassoon had noticed that young Hassun spoke with very good, educated Arabic, but whenever he digressed and wanted to say something about love, he borrowed his words from English or French, as if his Arabic could not cope with the subject. Furthermore, he spoke English with rather a soft American accent. Being a professor of medicine, the doctor could not resist enquiring after this strange phenomenon.

'Tell me, young man, you scatter your language with a lot of English words, rather sophisticated English words. Where have you learnt that, if I may ask?'

'I studied until recently at the Baghdad College. We were taught in English by American Jesuit fathers. My Arabic got mixed up. We studied Shakespeare and Dickens.'

'I understand.'

The two men shook hands and Dr Abdul Salam Sassoon saw the young man to the door where he was received by Nurse Victoria. There was, by this time, quite a crowd of pregnant women waiting impatiently for their turn. They looked at Hassun Abd al-Ali with apparent astonishment, a man emerging from a gynaecologist's surgery. 'Well, well! Everything is possible nowadays with modern medicine,' one of the women said to her companion.

'Indeed, they can do anything nowadays.'

'Sabiha Askar,' the nurse called for the next patient.

❦ 4 ❧

Hassun's Schooling

Like everywhere else, well-to-do families in the Middle East were in the habit of sending their children to be educated in private schools, preferably prestigious foreign schools, and engaging private tutors to help them in their studies, especially mathematics and English. These schools were usually attached to religious organizations and therefore pursued different syllabuses, in each case the emphasis being on the holy scriptures and religious instruction appropriate to their own learning and affiliation. There were a few such schools in Baghdad: Al-Ja'fariah Secondary School catering mostly for Shi'i Muslims, Al-Tafayyud School catering for Sunni Muslims, the American Secondary School and the Baghdad College catering for the Christians and the Alliance Israelite Universalle School and the Sham-mash School run by the Jews for the Jews but open to others. In addition there were smaller Jewish institutions like the Laura Kadoori School for Girls. Sayyid Abd al-Ali, a high-ranking civil servant in the Foreign Ministry, decided to send his eldest son, Hassun, to be educated at the Baghdad College, which was run by American Jesuits and had gained a high reputation in almost every field of learning and education. No segregation or discrimination was practised by the school administration or by the families of the pupils. Muslim children were often sent to Jewish or Christian schools, and Christian or Jewish pupils were sometimes sent to the state schools. The one segregation strictly observed was between boys and girls, whether Muslims, Christians or Jews. The only factor otherwise was that of money – what the family could afford. As Sayyid Muhammad Abd al-Ali was quite prosperous, he sent his oldest son to the most expensive establishment; that was Baghdad College.

Unlike almost all the other establishments which were actually large family houses converted into schools, the Baghdad College was a purpose-built educational institution with a proper sports ground, science laboratories, theatre and lecture hall. The administration and the teaching were mainly undertaken by the fathers themselves. The buildings occupied a suburban area surrounded by palm trees and orange groves near the Tigris River, known as al-Sulaikh, some fifteen miles from the centre of Baghdad. The boys were picked up by school coaches from certain points along the main streets on the north-east side of the city. As Hassun lived on the southern side, he had to walk, early in the morning, to one of the appointed stops. The coaches and their young passengers, in their spotlessly clean uniforms, shepherded by their American teachers dressed in white habits adorned by large silver crosses, were resented by the other natives who looked on them as a manifestation of Western imperialist domination and the harbingers of a new Christian crusade to convert the indigenous Muslims to Christianity.

True, the purpose of these missionary schools was to win converts to Christianity, but on the whole they achieved no tangible result in the Muslim world. The generous bounties and medical help they provided had won them a few converts among the marshland Arabs. The improvised school set up in the marshlands of the south regularly celebrated Christmas in the presence of the visiting bishop, head of the mission. The schoolmaster/father would describe all the miracles of the Son of God, concluding with Jesus walking on the Sea of Galilee, and was accustomed to hear his congregation of converts greet his story with one fervent voice, 'Oh, praise be to Muhammad!'

With the failure of the missionary work among the Muslim majority, the priests turned their attention to converting Christians of other sects: Orthodox Christians to Catholicism or ethnic Christians to Orthodoxy, and so on. To this, the missionary work of Baghdad College was reduced.

Apart from dwelling on the stories and teachings of the Bible, the school fathers taught the pupils the classics of English and American literature, with predictable emphasis on Shakespeare and the great Romantics with their moving love stories. One year, the school embarked on staging *Romeo and Juliet*, with the part of Juliet taken by one of the bright and handsome boys, who as it happened was none other than Hassun Abd al-Ali. The play made a deep impression on him, as it might on any adolescent boy or girl. He was in tears when the performance ended and he, as well as his companions, were cheered and clapped by the teachers, visitors and all their fellow students. For many days he was entranced, living and reliving the story and the fate of the hapless Romeo and his Juliet. Nothing like that had ever existed in Arabic literature or local folklore.

✄ 5 ✄

Boy Meets Girl

Sayyid Abd al-Ali was in the habit of swapping his daily newspaper, *al-Zaman*, for the newspaper of his friend Haj Nufal, the prestigious *al-Bilad*. It was always done in the evening when both gentlemen had finished with their own newspaper and when Hassun would be back from school to carry out this humble task of effecting the exchange. He would take *al-Zaman* from his father and deliver it to Abu Mamduh who in return would hand over his *al-Bilad*. It was Samira's little job to answer the door and see him out. It took only a matter of a few moments to exchange greetings and hand over the papers, but those few moments gave the young boy sufficient time to view the innocent beauty of his neighbour's daughter. She was of a light brown complexion, the colour of an English girl returning from a fortnight's holiday in Oman. Her chestnut hair, woven into a thick braid, hung heavily down her back. She certainly needed no mascara on her long eyelashes which danced to the lilt of her sweet voice and the gentle words of her young neighbour. As she was at home with her parents and two brothers, when Hassun

52

called she was dressed informally in a simple, low-necked dress, no more than a nightdress, of the sort that it was quite customary for women to wear at home in Iraq. This gave Hassun the chance to see more of her voluptuous body's finer points. Being a few inches taller than her, he was able to glimpse the pale colour of the top of her breasts, which dazzled his eyes and made him sigh inwardly. The young man's days were divided between the happy ones, which were sheer joy to remember, and the miserable ones, miserable enough to curse. It was a happy day whenever she answered his knock and a damned miserable day when it was one of her two brothers who came to the door.

As the days passed, the happy ones and the miserable ones, his form of greeting changed from a mere, 'Good-evening, sister,' to, 'Hello, Samira, keeping well?' Sometimes he asked her about her school work and how she was getting on with her maths. The lover spent his sleepless nights planning a daring venture – to waylay her on her morning journey to school on the other side of the river and speak to her. More sleepless nights were required to compose the right words.

'Good morning, Samira. What a coincidence, meeting you on my way to school.' No, that won't do. She would have seen that I was following her. It is also pompous.

Make it friendly and direct: 'Such heavy books you

are carrying, my dear Samira. May I help you with your load?' No, no! That would only work if she was really carrying a lot of heavy books, which was rare. It would take him weeks and months to have that lucky chance.

'Hello, dear Samira. Is it all right to walk with you?' That is too daring. What if she said no, don't walk with me? It would be all over.

Best thing is to ask her about the time. No! That would be an absurd question with the Qushla Tower Clock in front of us. She would think I was simple or retarded. Yet, on second thoughts, it would be a good question to make her laugh. Laughter is a good start for anything. She would know that I was desperate to speak to her. I would look at the Qushla Tower Clock and say to her, 'Hello, Samira. What is the time, I wonder?' He spent the rest of the night rehearsing and waiting for the hour when he could ask her about the hour.

The trick worked and she laughed, pointing to the Qushla Tower; this led on to speculation about the accuracy of the old Ottoman timepiece and its history. Was it really so accurate? Who maintained and repaired it? How did they wind it up and oil its machinery? 'Together with the Hindiah Dam and the Nazum Pasha Barrier, it is among the only worthy works left in Iraq by the Ottoman Turks,' Hassun pontificated and the young woman was clearly impressed by his knowledge of history. He allowed a few days to pass before trying a repetition of the ruse. This time the subject was the latest Egyptian romantic film being shown in the cinemas of Baghdad. The stratagem worked like the Qushla Tower Clock. The journey to school became a regular rendezvous, often extending well beyond the beginning of class as they stole for themselves more time to spend together wandering around the crowded Suq al-Kabir Bazaar, where they could not be easily detected. They looked like any young couple shopping for their wedding or choosing an engagement ring. Girls often wandered in that huge network of shops and stalls and endlessly winding lanes. It was the favourite haunt of all the gentle, female folk of Iraq. In that huge throng of diverse people, a young man might secretly hold the hand of his sweetheart or pinch the bottom of another man's wife.

Like most other great bazaars of the Middle East, the noisy and hectic Suq al-Kabir in al-Risafah, close to the Iraqi Museum and the old Mustansiriah University, was arranged on two floors. The ground floor was packed with little shops exhibiting goods and catering for customers, while the first floor afforded additional storage and office space to the shopkeepers below. Through one of his schoolmates, Hassun discovered that a certain carpet dealer in this bazaar was making his fortune not from buying and selling carpets, or from weaving them, but by hiring his well-secluded first-floor storeroom to frustrated lovers who had nowhere to go, no love nest to turn to, the eternal problem of lovers in the Middle East. For a mere two dirhams, a lover could bring his woman and enjoy an hour of intimacy on the expensive Tabriz or Kashan carpets. The room was adequately provided with light, water, soap and a good, secure lock. Hassun was properly introduced by Charles, his schoolmate, to the owner and manager of this worthy establishment. The arrangement proved to be very fruitful, convenient and affordable for a young student. Haj Mustafa, the carpet dealer, always cherished the visits of the young, educated couple. 'Enjoy yourself, young man, with God's blessing,' he used to salute Hassun as he entrusted him with the room's key. 'There is a jug of cold water in the fridge. And don't forget to draw the curtains properly and lock the door.'

The sweet, happy hours at the carpet store turned sour when Haj Nufal received a call from Samira's headmistress telling him of the repeated absences of his daughter from school and her failure to bring in any medical certificate or letter from her parents explaining her absence. The call couldn't have come in worse circumstances as the girl had started to complain of various physical symptoms and was off her food. It was time to take her on that fateful visit to Dr Abdul Salam Sassoon's clinic.

✿ 6 ✿

The Wanderer

Hassun did not go home the night after his sad visit to Dr Abdul Salam Sassoon's surgery. He reckoned that Samira's people would be after his blood to avenge the disgrace he had heaped on them and the loss of their daughter. His own parents would never forgive him and his father would give him a painful thrashing. The Baghdad College was sure to dismiss him forthwith and deny him access to the final baccalaureate examination. His tutor, Father Martin O'Connor, would be deeply angry at his misdeeds and the dishonour he had inflicted on the good name of the college. He would be, in short, a hunted man, disowned and avoided by all his relatives, friends and acquaintances. He certainly wouldn't be able to walk the streets of the Karkh district by day. Children would throw stones at him and sing abusive chants behind him. What was he to do? He spent the night trying to answer this question, wandering from street to street, from district to district, exhausted but unable to rest. He was stopped many times by the police and searched for any subversive leaflets or arms.

'Young man, it is late in the night. Go home before you get into mischief or come to some harm.'

'Thank you.'

His legs eventually took him to the sandy beaches of the Abu Nuwas Corniche by the Tigris River. At last, he threw himself on the clean, cold sand, hoping to sleep, but the stars above kept piercing his eyes with arrows of gleaming, silvery light. He covered his face with his palms to protect his sight against them. He turned away from the stars to his left and then to his right, hugging the folds of the innocent sand in despair. Prayers and verses of the Koran which he had long forgotten came back to his lips and the tip of his tongue. He prayed to the Almighty to forgive him, to save him, to light his way to a righteous path. With his face swimming in warm tears and shaken by convulsive sobs, he turned towards heaven and prayed: 'Oh God, forgive us our juvenile folly. Rest her soul in peace, if she is dead.'

The prayers restored some serenity to his soul and he closed his eyes and slept. But it was the same God who gave him peace and slumber who plucked them away from him again as the loudspeakers of the Firdaus Mosque awakened him to his sorrows with the call to the dawn prayer:

> God is greater,
> God is greater,
> Come to prayers,
> Come to the good work.

Hassun got up, shook the sand off his clothes and staggered back to the city of sin. The long and weary night became a day of toil. He passed Sadun Square, King Faisal II Square and finally reached Suq al-Safafir, the copper market. The sound of the beating of the copper plates and utensils assaulted his brain like hammers attacking him from every direction. As if he were a fugitive, he ran and ran as fast as he could, sometimes blocking his ears with his hands against the intolerable noise. He was relieved, at last, to find himself entering the great bazaar where he turned immediately in the familiar direction of the carpet dealer, Mustafa.

'What – so early in the morning? You lost your girl, eh?'

Receiving no answer, Haj Mustafa went on to tease the young man, 'Eh, somebody pinched her from you? What a shame! She was lovely. A schoolgirl! Never mind, you will find another. Schools are turning them out by the dozen.'

'Haj Mustafa, do you mind lending me your room for a couple of hours? I am exhausted and in need of some sleep. I have no money to pay you, though.'

The carpet dealer realised that some tragedy had taken place. 'What is it, my boy?' Hassun told him the full story and the old man revealed the boundless humanity of a carpet dealer. 'Here is the key. Sleep as much as you can. I won't allow anyone to use the room today.' Hassun took the key thankfully and went upstairs. He lay down on the same Tabriz carpet but he couldn't sleep; images of past happy hours with Samira haunted him, tears gushed from his eyes and he spent the day crying. When he was himself again, he saw by his side an old metal plate with two skewers of kebab, some parsley and a piece of pitta bread left for him by Haj Mustafa. There he stayed for two days, courtesy of the carpet dealer, until he began to feel that he had outstayed his welcome. The man had lost his income for two days and the users of the love nest were frustrated by his presence, and probably cursing him for it.

After thanking the old man for his kindness, Hassun directed his compass towards Sadun Street, in the forlorn hope of further news about Samira's fate from Dr Abdul Salam Sassoon. No such news was forthcoming and the doctor looked as stern as ever, but from him Hassun managed to secure somewhere to sleep for a few more days. Hearing of his plight, Dr Sassoon arranged for him to stay for a week in his clinic, leaving the practice in the morning and coming back in the evening when the last patient had gone. By way of further help, the good doctor gave him thirty-five dinars, the clinic's total earnings for the day, to tide him over this unhappy period, which Hassun received reluctantly but gratefully.

The week, however, passed slowly for the vagabond, who was forced to go back to his wandering existence, marching from pillar to post, from one district to another, always improvising for the night. He tried the benches of the West Baghdad Railway Station, but the station attendants turned him away, and the police would not allow him to sleep under the tall eucalyptus trees of the leafy Sadun Park. He tried to bed down on one of the benches along Abu Nuwas Street, but the traffic noise was too much and the electric lights too strong. Worse still, the cold and rainy winter season was setting in. With the rain, the river started to swell and thus to cover the sandy beaches, depriving the homeless of this free God-sent mattress for all. He followed their track to Baghdad's extensive cemeteries, of which he selected the central one, the Bab al-Mu'addam Cemetery, which had a little dome in the middle and accommodated many sacred martyrs, including the commander-in-chief of the Iraqi armed forces, Bakr Sidqi, who was killed by one of his officers in revenge for Sidqi's killing of his own commander-in-chief. There Hassun took himself one cold December night. It was pouring with rain and the young man had to seek cover under the tinplate canopy over one of the martyrs' graves. That saved him from the rain at the price of enduring the pitter-patter of the rain-drops beating on the thin metal canopy all through the night.

The cemetery caretaker almost died himself – of fright – in the morning, when he saw a man stretched out full length under the canopy. Allah be praised, he thought, it must be the dead martyr deciding to lie on rather than under the earth.

'No, sir! Certainly not. This is no place for the living to sleep. Only the dead are allowed to take their repose here.'

'But you are sleeping here.'

'Yes, we are cemetery keepers. We are here to look after the dead and protect them from people like you.'

The argument went backwards and forwards as to the right of the living to lie down in a graveyard before their proper time was due. The clash of words brought in another man in dirty vest and underwear, who emerged from the central tomb where a revered imam was buried with a blue dome all to himself. The man in his underwear walked forward until he was face to face with Hassun. 'I am Muhsin Abu Rass, the chief gravedigger here. You speak to me. I decide who may or may not be allowed to lie down here.'

Hassun explained his problem, that he had no money and no place to go to. The chief gravedigger had a closer look at Hassun. He walked all around him, examining his physique and features carefully, and then smiled, winked and turned to Hamad Awda, the cemetery keeper: 'Yes. The young man may stay with us. Give him a mattress and a blanket. Come, my lad, and have breakfast with us. What is your name?'

'Abdullah,' Hassun answered him circumspectly.

'Come along, Abdullah, and have something to eat and some tea to drink.' Hassun, alias Abdullah, followed his benefactor to the dome where he partook of a breakfast of sticky dates and thick yoghurt, washed down with a glass of black tea. He could not believe his good luck, for all things are relative. A night in a cemetery with a roof over your head is certainly better than a night on a wooden bench with no roof at all. Furthermore, these gravediggers were certainly more civilized than the Iraqi police. He ate his breakfast, washed his hands, relieved himself behind one of the better built graves and spent the day recovering from the turmoil of the past few days. In the evening, the chief gravedigger came back from town with a bottle of arak and a few oranges and pickled cucumbers. Hamad Awda put on the oil stove and boiled some salted chickpeas for meze. They ate, drank and chatted merrily about bizarre burials that they had experienced recently. Before turning in, and as they got tipsy, the oldest of them started to sing hoarsely the song of the gravediggers, with the rest joining in as a chorus :

> To sing or to cry, as I think and believe,
> Will not help the singer or the crier.
> O my friend, step lightly on this earth,
> For its crust is but the remains of the dead,
> One corpse heaped on another,
> Grinning at the congestion of their bones.

Hassun grinned, wrapped himself in the dirty, frayed blanket, curled up and dropped off to sleep immediately like a log. The oil lamp was blown out by Hamad Awda and silence pervaded the shrine, except for the noise of two of the gravediggers who were engaged in a snoring dialogue,

Only a few minutes had passed when Hassun was awakened by somebody trying to creep in beside him and pull down his trousers. He pulled them up again and pushed the intruding arm away, but the attempt was repeated, this time with more determination and force. It did not take long for Hassun to realize that he was in the midst of a rape attempt. The ensuing battle aroused the other sleepers, who roared with laughter, finding the contest immensely amusing. Some started to shout and encourage, others gave directions and even tried to help by holding Hassun's head or pinning down his arms and legs.

'Hamid, grab his head and hold it tight for me!'

'Ya, ya, but you hold him by his bottom!'

Hassun fought back hard and managed to land a direct kick in the chief digger's testicles which made him scream with pain and double over, swearing and shouting. 'This is the reward for my kindness. Give a man sanctuary and that is what you get! You give him food and shelter and he won't allow you a bit of fun in return.'

Hassun didn't make any comment, but collected himself, zipped up his trousers and walked out of the humble shrine. With the help of a distant street light, he managed to find himself a secure corner between the gravestones where he curled up and spent the night shivering and soaked by the rain. To this same corner he retreated every subsequent evening and spent the nights uncomfortably but peacefully. The cold which kept him awake elicted memories of happier days with Samira. His eyes filled with tears. Could she be still alive somewhere? If so, why didn't she try to contact him? No, they had killed her. That is what people are saying. They took her to the Jew doctor and then killed her. Where is she buried? Could she be buried here in this cemetery? Somewhere in an unmarked grave? Maybe I am lying on top of her right here!

Images of her appeared in his mind's eye. Glorious in her naked body, holding her firm teenage breasts like a couple of new tennis balls, laughing and seductive. Samira on her way to school, carrying her books and sports kit. Beside him on the days when they used to walk the big bazaar, hand in hand, her tender fingers tiny in his grasp, inviting him to snatch any opportunity to steal a fleeting kiss on her slender neck, her glowing cheeks or her slim arms. With his dirty hands, he wiped the tears from his cheeks, turned on his side and hugged the cemetery earth.

During the day, he went out into the city to look for food, rummaging in the refuse heaps outside restaurants and cafés, knocking on the doors of houses. 'Alms for Allah! Food for the hungry!' Some housewives took pity on him and gave him something to eat. Others were less kind. 'Go away! What is the matter with you?' At the street corner outside the imposing Iraqi Museum, he joined the line of beggars, women with their children in rags, blind old men reciting verses from the Holy Koran, cripples, children, war widows, and war heroes on crutches, all shouting and appealing and trying their best to touch the hearts of the passing pedestrians. They did not like the face of this new addition or his accent. 'You are not a deserving beggar. There is nothing wrong with you. Get lost.' Another, with a kinder disposition, was less severe in his words. 'Look here, young man, why don't you go to Abu Hanifa's shrine. There is better business there. People give money there. I wish I could walk like you and take myself there.' Hassun realized that there was nothing for it but to go back to the Bab al-Mu'addam Cemetery. There the gravediggers treated him as a pitiful reject of society but left him to his own devices. Sometimes they gave him a share of the charity food, mainly pastries, distributed by the bereaved families for the souls of the departed. Hamad Awda, was particularly kind to him and did his best to make him comfortable wherever he was, giving him a blanket, a jug of water, some of the food they had cooked and so on. One day he approached him with a proposal: 'Why don't you join us?'

'What do you mean?'

'Be one of us. Work with us as a gravedigger. There is a lot of money in it. People are dying here all the time. Those who don't die from tuberculosis are killed in the war. You are strong. I saw how you fought off our chief. You were the only one who managed to stop him. None of us could. He has raped every single one of us. Come and join us. Maybe one day, God willing, you will be our chief and you wont rape us as Muhsin Abu Rass is doing.'

The idea sounded tempting. Instead of living off people's charity, live by burying them. Not bad at all. The proposal was put to the chief and he accepted it readily. He was in need of a younger gravedigger with muscle and firm sinews for this back-breaking job. Hassun joined the gang on his own terms. A special place was cleared for him inside the shrine, and they brought him a new mattress, or almost new, with woollen blankets of a similar standard from the estate of a couple who had fallen into the open sewer of Bab al-Shaikh and died. He and the chief grave-digger became good friends once they had arrived at a mutual understanding. Muhsin Abu Rass enjoyed listening to the anecdotes and thrilling yarns narrated to him about all the exciting wonders of the world and revelled in bloody accounts of Islamic history, while for his part he told Hassun some of his own experiences from his long and colourful life: 'Listen, Abdullah, my friend, treat this cemetery as your own home. You may do anything you like in this place, but take my advice, don't ever bring a female here. Women are nothing but trouble.'

⚜ 7 ⚜

A Military Solution

Abd al-Ali's household had been in turmoil since the disappearance of their favourite son, Hassun. His mother had sunk into a mysterious yet understandable psychosomatic illness of which a notable side-effect was the constant nagging of her husband. It was all his fault. He had no idea how to bring up a boy. 'Why did you send him to a Catholic school? That was where he learned all that stuff about love and falling in love. He wanted to become another Romeo in al-Mishahdah. A Karkhi Romeo! I ask you!'

'My dear woman, I wanted him to learn English. It just happened that *Romeo and Juliet* is an English story. It is not my fault that these stupid fathers did not choose some other more decent story. Had they chosen the adventures of Robin Hood, he would probably have become a gangster. That is what happens when you teach children things which are not home grown.'

Mrs Abd al-Ali remained unconvinced. It was all the fault of her man. At every meal, the same husband-and-wife argument started. If it was stuffed chicken with almonds, that would cause another bout of crying. 'Oh, Hassun used to like his stuffed chicken with almonds.' A similar storm of tears occurred if the dish was okra with lamb, minced kebab with pickles, kibba with beetroot salad or any of the popular Iraqi dishes. 'Oh, Hassun used to like this . . . Hassun used to love that.'

'If you were a man and a true husband and father, you would go and find him. What has happened to him? Has he been killed by Samira's brothers, in revenge? Has he committed suicide like that fellow Romeo did?'

The man actually did what he could to track down his son, but although he left no stone unturned or schoolmate uncontacted he could find no trace of him, not until that day when he joined his friends and colleagues in attending the funeral of Dr Saad Bahri, the director-general of the Ministry of Social Affairs, who had died of syphilis and cirrhosis of the liver. At the edge of the freshly dug grave, he saw his son, looking rough and unshaven, in a tatty shirt and worn-out trousers and holding an old rusty spade in his hand, ready to shovel the earth over his friend, Dr Bahri. Sayyid Abd al-Ali rubbed his eyes in disbelief. Nothing could have persuaded him to accept even a remote possibility of his cherished son, student of the Baghdad College, turning into a common grave-digger were it not for the evidence of his own eyes.

He controlled himself and pretended not to have seen Hassun, let alone recognized him. Patiently he waited and calmly dispersed with the rest of the mourners. 'May the Almighty God help you with your sorrow,' he murmured as he shook hands with the sons and brothers of the deceased.

What was he to do now? How had his son, brought up and educated at considerable cost and with great effort to be a minister, a judge or a doctor, sunk to the level of working as a gravedigger with the riff-raff of Iraqi society at half a dinar per grave? He realized that the transformation was far too profound to be reversed by mere words or gentle persuasion. Besides, what was the alternative? Were he to abandon the company of the dead and the derelict, where would he go? Would he be safe anywhere from the vengeance of Haj Nufal's tribe? Would they not subject him to every possible act of humiliation? All the way back to his home, Sayyid Abd al-Ali pondered these and other questions. By the parapet of King Faisal's Bridge, he stopped and contemplated the thirty-metre drop to the water. How easy it would be to jump over and free himself from this abject disgrace and oppressive anxiety! Wouldn't it be a really good solution? He brooded, and raised his head in melancholy, and looked at the distant bend of the river. To his left, on the Karkh side of the Tigris, stood the Qamariah Mosque, with its dwarf minaret of bricks reflected on the calm water against the palm trees behind. The occasional ripple disturbed the picture and twisted all its outlines. The minaret's reflection shimmered and danced softly whenever a rowing boat ferrying passengers passed by, the boatman singing a *pasta* loudly as he moved his entire body forwards and backwards in the effort of pulling and pushing at the oars. A blast from a military trumpet sounded and turned Abd al-Ali's head in the opposite direction. The flag at the Ministry of Defence on the Risafah side of the river was being lowered and the soldiers were standing in salute. It was the end of the day for them. Sayyid Abd al-Ali watched the solemn occasion as the soldiers marched back to their barracks, rifles on shoulders. He followed them with his eyes as they disappeared behind the pale eucalyptus trees, carrying themselves rigidly erect in due respect for the ceremony, unperturbed by its daily repetition. Hassun's father raised himself from the iron parapet and resumed his journey home, but now with a gentle smile on his face and fresh thoughts in his mind.

It was a sweet-and-sour-flavoured story that Mrs Abd al-Ali heard from her husband. She smiled and frowned, for the sweet side was the discovery of her wayward son but the sour side was the remedy for his redemption.

'I know of only one solution for this fellow: the army. Nothing can cure an errant boy's wild conduct better than military service. Two years in the Iraqi infantry will be sufficient to drive the most stubborn genies from his head.'

Early the following morning, Sayyid Abd al-Ali drove to the Ministry of Defence and sought the Directorate of Military National Service, where he found the conscription officer in charge of his area.

'Sayyid Abd al-Ali, I am glad of your visit. To tell you the truth, since his disappearance from school, I have had the name of your boy on my list of army deserters. I didn't know what to do about it. I couldn't really humiliate myself by troubling a man of your distinction, Sayyid Abd al-Ali, and abusing his house. It is not easy to send a couple of military policemen to force their way into the house and grab the bugger by the scruff of his neck. But now that you are telling me to do just that, my men are more than eager to perform this act. Nothing gives more pleasure to the military police than finding hands to fit their handcuffs!'

'Thank you, officer. But the trouble is that you won't find him in our house.'

'Don't you worry about that, your excellency. We know where these buggers go. They always end up in a cemetery. But in most cases long before the time appointed by the Almighty.' The officer chuckled, proud of this little bit of military humour.

'You are right, officer. And how true! Now to save you from any unnecessary search, I can tell you that you will find him in the Bab al-Mu'addam Cemetery.'

'Yes, it is their favourite place. Very central and close to the Kallachiah Brothel.'

Both men shared a hearty laugh and Sayyid Abd al-Ali, having finished his glass of tea, left the conscription office and departed from the Ministry of Defence flushed with success.

Squatting on the marble slab of a grave, covered with dust, Hassun was eating his lunch of dates, yoghurt and bread with his fellow gravediggers when four military policemen entered the cemetery and walked purposefully towards them. He made no attempt to run away as he thought that they were coming with another order for a fresh grave, duly earned by and needed for one more martyr. There was a little civil war somewhere in the north and the martyrs were coming regularly, much to the satisfaction of the gravediggers and cemetery attendants.

'Sayyid Hassun bin Sayyid Abd al-Ali, you are under arrest,' barked Sergeant Latif, the officer in charge. Hassun jumped from the grave, threw away his dates and tried to run for it, but the four ablebodied soldiers were too much for him. One soldier held his arms tight while another fitted the handcuffs around his wrists and the third led him away. 'Give him a good kick,' shouted the sergeant-major and Hassun duly received it on his backside. He limped, but walked faster.

'What a shame! He was such a good gravedigger,' mumbled Hamad the cemetry caretaker.

'Yeah! And well educated. There is nothing he doesn't know.'

'We're sure going to miss him.'

The military police walked him between the crumbling gravestones to the military vehicle waiting outside the gate and drove him straight away to the headquarters of the Fourth Infantry Division at al-Rashid Military Base, east of Baghdad. There, his details were checked, his medical condition examined, his hair shaved off and a conscript's uniform was measured up for him. Finally, he was issued with a shiny pair of black army boots. In less than an hour, he was a new man, a new soldier ready to fight and die for God, king and country.

'Here you are a soldier. Remember that always. You do what you are told, not what you think you want to do. We know all about you. We even know how many hairs you have in your arse. This is no place for any monkey business or horseplay, you hear, Hassun ibn Abd al-Ali?'

'Yes, sir.'

'You polish your shoes and clean your equipment before you go to bed. Five in the morning you must be up and ready for the morning run. You hear?'

'Yes, sir.'

'Dismissed.'

Hassun made a salute, turned smartly on his heel and left the office. He endured the infantry discipline for a week, but the weekend rest put an early end to this trial. Once more, he sought shelter among the dead in a cemetery, this time the Sheikh

Omar Cemetery to the north of the capital, which surrounded the Bab al-Wastani Military Museum with its graves and humble shrines.

This was an open Muslim burial ground close to the Jewish Cemetery. For centuries past, the dead of the two great monotheistic faiths had lived happily next to each other without any problem. The Jewish Cemetery, however, was surrounded by a brick wall, some two meters high, with only one gateway, normally shut. It dawned on Hassun that perhaps living among the dead Jews would be safer for him, and he knocked at the gate to enquire whether they needed a gravedigger. No one answered his call. He climbed over the wall and looked among the graves for a suitable place for himself. Jewish tombs had no tinplate canopies over them and the only protection against the weather was behind the large semi-cylindrical monument commemorating the Shavuot Pogrom of 1941, better known as the Farhud Massacre, in which the Baghdadi mob attacked the poorer Jews in their ancient localities around al-Shurja, Abu Sayfin and Suq Hannoun, following the Rashid Ali military débâcle against Britain.

He wondered as he lay down by its side, how many people were buried there beneath him? Fifty, as the authorities claimed, or two hundred, as the Jews said? The idle question unsettled his mind. All through the night, visions of the victims appeared to him in his dreams, women stripped naked, bearded rabbis, children crawling on their stomachs, babies screaming, the blind and disabled begging for their clothes. Some were laughing hysterically, others shrieking or begging for mercy, all running for their lives hither and thither. He joined them in their shrieking. He screamed and woke himself up, terrified, but the monumental Jewish tomb remained silent There was silence everywhere. Hassun was shaken and too frightened to sleep again. He sat up, leaning with his back against the simple brick-and-mortar monument, with drops of sweat gathering on his forehead, hot and moist. More ghastly images floated before his eyes and screamed in his ears, as he shivered and hugged his shaking body. It was cold – so was the night.

He resolved to climb back into the Muslim cemetery where he would be more at home and where he might be able to sleep within the shrine of Sheikh Omar and enjoy the luxury of a roof over his head. At least he wouldn't see those apparitions or hear the screams of frightened women and children. Perhaps, he could also offer his services to the attendant as an experienced gravedigger and thereby gain reasonable employment. Surely his previous employer at the Bab al-Muaddam Cemetery would give him a good reference?

Just as he came over the wall, an army vehicle drew nearer and a bunch of military police jumped out and ran after him. 'Where will you go? You had better stop, my lad. There is no way for you to escape. We'll hound you to the ends of the earth.' They were right, he thought, and lost the will to run any farther. They gave him an instant lesson of half a dozen blows and mighty kicks before dragging him into their vehicle. He was given a summary trial and was sentenced to thirty lashes on his bare bottom in front of his entire platoon, assembled purposely for this public demonstration of corporal punishment. He was then taken on a cart to serve one week of solitary confinement.

When, however, the harshness of the penalty did not deter him from repeating the experience twice more, his commanders decided to try a more lasting punishment and at the same time get rid of him once and for all. 'The trouble,' Captain Walid decided, 'is that Baghdad is too good for his like. They find lots of fun and diversion here. There are too many cemeteries in this city. That is what I have always believed. Too many cemeteries where men can take their women or young boys and enjoy themselves. The government should do away with them. One big cemetery, well guarded and inspected, should be enough.'

It was, therefore, decided to exile Hassun Abd al-Ali to Jordan and add him to the Iraqi Expeditionary Force sent there to bolster the forces of the brotherly Jordanian Armed Forces in the impending war against the Jews of Palestine.

'Private Hassun, go home today, say goodbye to your parents, collect your things and report tomorrow, sometime in the morning, to the transport department. We'll be glad to see the end of you and good riddance.'

'I hope you will learn some discipline from the Jordanians,' added First Lieutenant Faisal Abbud Husni.

Hassun was thus kicked out of the Rashid Military Base. He went home, kissed his father and apologised to him for all the trouble and disappointment that he had caused the family. His mother baked him a quantity of *kalicha* pastries with dates, nuts and sugar. She packed them for him together with a few of his things. 'Just a moment,' he called, and dashed upstairs only to come back with one more item to add to his baggage – his copy of *Romeo and Juliet*. As he left the house, he turned round to wave to his mother. She was at the door pouring out a bucket of water in his direction – a traditional ritual for ensuring good luck and safe journeys.

There was just one more thing for him to do. He must go to Sadun Street and bid farewell to Dr Abdul Salam Sassoon. Perhaps the doctor might, this time, have some news for him about the fate of his beloved. 'Doctor Salam must know a great deal about what happened to her, but he just won't tell me.' Hassun still had some time before he had to report to his officer. He took a bus to Bistan al-Khass and walked, with his things, to the clinic. 'The doctor is no longer here,' the butcher shouted to him, only to receive a wry smile from the conscript in uniform. Yet there was, indeed, a notice on the door confirming the butcher's assertion: THIS CLINIC IS CLOSED UNTIL FURTHER NOTICE. It seemed strange but true.

He tried the door anyway and found it was not locked. He pushed it open and saw a light shining upstairs. He heard the sound of a typewriter. He ventured up the stairs and found no other than Nurse Victoria at her desk.

'Oh, hello, what has brought you here today? And, bless me, all in military uniform! A soldier on the way to war!'

'What is going on here? What is this notice on the door? Where is Dr Abdul Salam?'

'Oh, you haven't heard? Dr Abdul Salam, I am sorry to say, has lost his wits. He is now certified as insane.'

In the wake of that fateful visit from the Haj Nufal duo, he had begun to develop physical and mental problems, seeing things and hearing voices – imagining blood everywhere. He would scream and take a knife to defend himself. He wouldn't drink or eat because he thought there was blood in his food and drink.

'Can I see him anywhere?'

'No, you can't. He is now kept at the Shamma'iah

Mental Asylum with strict orders from his doctor that no one should be allowed to visit him. Not even his wife or myself, his secretary. I am only here to look after his papers and wind up his practice. All these poor women who were relying on him – what a calamity! What a tragedy!'

Hassun was aghast. He felt short of breath, his chest grew tight and tears pricked his eyes. Poor Dr Abdul Salam Sassoon. The young man retraced his steps back through the waiting-room without saying goodbye to the nurse. He looked at the paintings which Abdul Salam Sassoon had hung on the walls and walked out.

'Didn't I tell you? That bloody Jew doctor went nuts,' Saudi, the butcher, chortled as he wiped his thick moustache with his greasy hand.

❦ 8 ❧

Not Quite Right

Tiffaha Sassoon had noticed a change in her husband's behaviour, a change for the worse. He would be smiling and looking pleased with life at one moment and sinking into gloom and despondency at the next. It was a hard job for her to coax him into eating anything, even when she tried to cook for him one of his favourite dishes – the tabbit chicken, the mahasha of stuffed peppers, the kichree of rice and red lentils or any other of Iraqi's Jewish delicacies. Late at night she would find him in the living-room, in his pyjamas, large kitchen knife in hand, looking frightened and anxious. 'Get out! Get out! I didn't kill her . . . I didn't! I didn't!' she heard him screaming one night. On another night she could find no trace of him anywhere in the house. She searched for him in the kitchen, in the garden, on the flat roof of the building, but she could see no sign of him. He had simply walked all the way, some four kilometres, barefoot and in his vest and pyjama trousers, to his surgery where he was found the following day by his secretary fast asleep on the examination couch.

The problem became more acute and his condition

the talk of the town when the police called one day and arrested him, accusing him of molesting the wife of a corn merchant who had come to him for an antenatal examination. The charge was amicably dropped when the woman and her husband realized the mental state he was in. 'I advise you, madam, to take him straight away to a good psychiatrist before he commits a more serious crime or does some harm to himself. He may even start attacking you,' the police officer intimated privately to Mrs Tiffaha Sassoon.

She followed the officer's advice and took her husband to Dr Jack Abbudi, the well-known Jewish psychiatrist, at the Royal Hospital in Baghdad. After listening to his story, Dr Abbudi came to the conclusion that his paranoia stemmed from that fateful encounter with the brothers, Mamduh and Ahmad, and the surgical operation he had had to perform all by himself on the young girl. It had been too much for his sensitive, artistic nature. A course of twelve ECT sessions were prescribed, together with a massive dose of tablets, which were, in fact, no more than strong sleeping pills which left Dr Abdul Salam Sassoon a zombie for most of the time. Dr Abbudi's prescription helped the patient only slightly for a couple of months before he sank into a more serious state of extreme anxiety which left him shaking and shivering. Another psychiatrist was recommended to them – Dr Wolfe of the Meir Elias Jewish Hospital, west of Baghdad in the Aywadiyya district. It was a pleasant, small medical establishment with a large central garden flourishing with orange, lemon, pomegranate and palm trees, around which the various clinics, wards and laboratories were situated. The hospital was a charitable institution, offering free treatment for the Jewish poor and a service for fee-paying patients from the rest of the community – Jews, Christians and Muslims alike. Most of the medics were either local Jewish doctors or those imported from Europe. Among the latter group was Dr Wolf, who hailed from Vienna and emigrated to Iraq, escaping the anti-Semitic onslaught in Austria in the wake of Hitler's invasion of the country in 1938.

Dr Wolfe's remedy, a mixture of counselling and psychoanalysis, produced no tangible results either and the poor Doctor Abdul Salam Sassoon was eventually committed to the Shamma'iyya Mental Asylum, north-east of the city. It was hoped that isolation from annoyances and daily psychiatric attention might help him to recover his wits sufficiently to restore him to normal life in his home and practice.

Late in 1947, the United Nations decided to partition Palestine into two states, one for the Jews and one for the Arabs. This resolution was followed accordingly in May 1948 by the establishment of the state of Israel, which prompted the Arab armies, including those of Iraq, to attack it forthwith. This was the curtain raiser to an hysterical anti-Semitic campaign waged against the hundred and thirty thousand Jews of Iraq, during which every single Jew was suspected of sympathy with Israel and spying for it. One daily newspaper, *al-Yagdha*, embarked on publishing lists and lists of Jews who were in the employment of the government or receiving benefits from it, saying that they should all be sacked, if not actually arrested and put behind bars as suspect citizens. In this atmosphere of hysteria, the authorities had no option but to accede. Every time the Arab armies suffered a reverse of fortune, the screw was turned tighter on the local Jews. Those who tried to raise a more sober voice and defend them were accused of pandering to the enemies and were lumped together as 'ikhwan al-Yahud' (brothers of the Jews). The country went quite off its head with rampant anti-Semitism.

In the house of the mad, the Shamma'iyya Mental Asylum, it was a question of the mad set upon by the twice as mad. The inmates threw stones and orange peel at Dr Abdul Salam Sassoon, the 'bloody Zionist spy'. 'How come that one of the clever Jews is put in a mental home as a madman? He must surely be a spy dressed as a lunatic to listen to what we say and report it to Israel,' one of the saner madmen concluded.

The administration was divided as the accountant questioned the validity of spending public money on

the upkeep of a Jew. The local paper published a
poem by a nationalist bard satirising Arab govern-
ments and Muslim ministers who spent the people's
money on looking after Zionist stooges while denying
the same privilege to umpteen Muslim lunatics who
roamed the streets of Baghdad with no home to go
to. Dr Adnan Ismail, the managing director of the
asylum, had no choice but to cover himself and his
position by getting rid of this one solitary Jew. But
he was kind enough to call for Mrs Tiffaha Sassoon
and explain to her the situation.

'This is no longer a place for your husband to get
better, with these inmates throwing stones at him
and pissing on his food. Best thing is to take him
home and isolate him from the rest of the people until
God lifts this black cloud hovering over all of us.'

Dr Ismail had the discharge certificate already
signed and stamped in duplicate, testifying that
the man had completely recovered his sanity. Tiffaha
Sassoon thanked him for his help and drove her
husband home to al-Karrada al-Sharqia, accompanied by one of the asylum's attendants to make
sure that he didn't go anywhere else.

Relatives and friends who visited the family
advised Tiffaha to change course and seek the help
of the divine. They were not short of evidence and
anecdotes supporting the superiority of spiritual
power over temporal power. Each one of them came
forth with some story of an afflicted mortal who was

given up by the medics only to be saved by the rabbis. There was Salma, Isaac's young daughter, who had third-degree tuberculosis and was given up for dead, but one touch by Hakham Khadduri cured her of her illness so that she went on to get married and produce five children, all boys. Although sceptical by nature and secular by education, Mrs Sassoon was prevailed upon to try the magic of Hakham Eliaho, a Baghdadi rabbi reputed to have had special success in curing mental afflictions. A certain David Ben Nasir gave up the career of shoemaking, his father's and grand-father's noble craft, to learn to sing the traditional *maqam* and play the juza, an ancient instrument; but Hakham Eliaho prescribed a certain verse from the Torah to be repeated a hundred times by his wife, and the man was restored to his senses and went back to his father's shop in Souk Hinnouni, where he was making excellent shoes again in no time. Hakham Eliaho's miraculous works were cited even by his Muslim and Christian neighbours, who often took their indisposed children to him for a charm or a prayer.

Hakham Eliaho looked tall and impressive, with a large round face and white complexion. Iraqi Jewry, whose ancestors were taken by Nebuchadnezzar in captivity to Babylon and kept apart for some two thousand five hundred years, probably represent the most pure sample of the Jewish gene. Yet the Middle Eastern male obsession with white flesh and a fair complexion resulted, in consequence of the centuries' long unnatural selection of pale-skinned females, in fair Jews with un-Semitic features, at least among the rich and the well-to-do from whose ranks the revered rabbi had emerged. To him, Tiffaha took her suffering husband, together with some gifts of manna and halek. The rabbi, with his long white beard, traditional embroidered kaftan and round headgear, listened patiently to the woman's account. Dr Abdul Salam Sassoon kept silent, wondering what had brought him thither and what business he, a confirmed atheist, had with this man of God. 'It is no good prescribing something for him to recite,' Tiffaha said. 'He won't do it. He is a non-believer. Give him something to drink or carry in his pocket.'

The rabbi took hold of the doctor by the arm and read something, facing towards him. He then produced a piece of paper, wrote something on it and gave it to Mrs Sassoon. 'Put this in his jacket whenever you can, but don't fight him over it.'

She nodded and took the scrap of paper and put it in her handbag. She thanked the man of God, left a one-dinar note on the table and departed with her husband, whose eyes still looked glazed but who managed, none the less, to say goodbye to the old man in the robe.

Days passed but no appreciable improvement was noticed in Dr Sassoon's condition or behaviour. He kept repeating, 'No! No! I did not kill her. I did not . . . I did not.' Without anyone understanding what he meant or to whom he was referring, they could only keep on wondering and guessing.

The gardener, a good Muslim from Kurdistan, who had been engaged by Abdul Salam Sassoon and was treated kindly by the family, decided to give Mrs Sassoon a bit of advice. 'Madam, I see how you are suffering because of the state of mind the master is in. I know you are Jews and I am a Muslim, but many Jews and Christians – all sorts of people and believers – seek the help of Mullah Jawad, a Kurd from Sulaymaniah. He is a Muslim healer but he has cured so many people, Kurds and Arabs. That is why they go to him. You won't lose anything by visiting him. A few dirhams will be sufficient for the mullah. He may not even take that when he knows whom he is treating – the great doctor of women, Dr Abdul Salam Sassoon. You won't lose anything by calling on him.'

Indeed not. How could they lose anything by talking to a cleric with a turban and a white beard. The gardener gave her directions to his place. Mullah Jawad lived in the Fadhil district near the Bab al-Mu'addam railway station. 'You can't miss it as there is a little stable by the side of the house for the use of people who might come on horseback or donkey. The mullah himself has his horse there, fully saddled and ready for any emergency use, so to speak. There is even a copy of the Koran, well bound, stashed by the right side of the saddle.' Before going to that strange destination in this very strong Muslim area, well known for its nationalistic learning and responsible for much of the bloody slaughter of Jews in the Shavuot Pogrom – the Farhud Massacre of 1941, Tiffaha Sassoon contacted her sister Zulaikha and her cousin, Professor Hakim. Yes, they said to her, Mullah Jawad is a respectable cleric and is often visited by Jews and followers of all faiths in Iraq.

Convincing herself of the advisability of this errand was one thing but persuading her husband was another. Though defective in mind he was, neverthe-less, becoming impatient with all this talk of divine deliverance. She had to use all her female powers to coax her husband into agreeing to come with her to the hated Fadhil district. The mullah received them kindly. After offering them some strong Turkish coffee, he listened to her account.

'Yes, yes, madam. You say that he keeps referring to this matter of killing. Yes, it is clear that what we have here is the work of the devil. Pure and simple. Curse be upon him. Wherever you hear of killing, you know that there the devil has been at work. But we know how to deal with him. God gave us reason and the Holy Koran with which to fight him.'

The mullah got up, pushed his white turban back and went across to Dr Sassoon. He stood behind him, bending over him, then putting his hands on either side of his head he began to recite verses of Surat al-Nas:

In the name of God, the merciful and
                            compassionate,
I seek refuge with the Lord,
The Ruler of mankind,
The God of mankind,
From the mischief of the whisperer,
Who whispers into the hearts of mankind
Among the jinn and among men.

The mullah then blessed the head of the Jew with his hand and went back to his desk. He opened a drawer from which he took an amulet with some letters and signs on it. He picked up his pen and scribbled a few more signs. That done, the mullah put the amulet in an envelope, sealed it and gave it to Mrs Sassoon. 'Put this under his pillow every evening before he goes to bed. With the help of Allah, you should see an improvement in his condition. Bless you, my dear sister.' Tiffaha Sassoon thanked him for his work, put a dinar on his desk and was about to lead her husband out of this place of spiritual healing, when Mullah Jawad put out his hand and stopped her to whisper these words into her ear: 'If his condition persists, you should take him to al-Kifil, to the tomb of your prophet Ezekiel. He is your prophet and our prophet. His miracles are countless. Take him there if needs be!'

Mrs Sassoon thanked him once more for his advice and departed. She conscientiously observed Mullah

Jawad's instructions, putting the amulet under Abdul Salam's pillow every night, but no improvement in her husband's condition was noticed, not by herself nor by anyone else. The trip to the Fadhil district had been a waste of time and money but Tiffaha remembered the mullah's advice and his mention of the prophet Ezekiel. She gave it further thought and decided to consult Hakham Eliaho once more.

She took a horse-drawn carriage to Aqd al-Yahud in old Baghdad and walked to the Great Synagogue, Slat li-Kbiri. The building was cast in the typical style of a Baghdadi house of the period, with a spacious central courtyard surrounded by large *iwans* and the worshipping-rooms housing the *tik*, the Torah case of decorative silver overlaid on wood, and some seventy scrolls. The high roofs of the *iwans*, the large alcoves, were supported by tall and simple hexagonal columns, barely one foot in diameter, made of wood and crowned with decorative capitals, also made of wood. The largest of these *iwans*, the main *hechal* (ark) contained the Sifrei Torch. Low wooden railings surrounded the short stairs leading to it. With no marble, stone or hard wood in the immediate vicinity of Baghdad, the whole synagogue was built with simple, baked bricks in the Islamic style, with painted arches and decorative motifs based on ten-point stars. Of course, no paintings or pictures of any kind were to be found. The whole thing looked austere, simple and unostentatious. There was nothing to come between the worshipper and God.

Tiffaha Sassoon knocked at the large wooden door and was soon admitted to the open courtyard where she found Hakham Eliaho perched on a traditional *takhat*, a long and high settee made of soft wood and covered with a thin mattress and a Persian carpet. The rabbi closed the voluminous book he was reading and stood up to welcome his visitor and invite her to sit at the other end of the *takhat*. She told him of her visit to Mullah Jawad and the advice that she had received from him to go and seek the help of the prophet Ezekiel.

'Yes, Mullah Jawad is a good man. He advised you well, my daughter. Go by all means to al-Kifil. It is near the city of Hilla and the ruins of Babylon. It is only a short trip, by car, from Baghdad, barely a two-hour drive. You can stay in a small hotel attached to the shrine. I shall provide you with a letter to our man there, Shammash Menashi Fagiro. He is a good *mekubal* and will do his best for the doctor.'

Tiffaha Sassoon pursed her lips and resolved to take her husband there, come what may.

❧ 9 ❧

Time with Ezekiel

Neither Dr Sassoon nor his wife were practising Jews or interested in religious matters. Taking her husband to these men of God was to Mrs Sassoon a matter of last resort. She had heard of the little town of al-Kifil and the prophet Ezekiel buried there but her knowledge did not extend beyond the geographical location, which was in central Iraq by the Euphrates River, close to the Muslim holy cities of Najaf and Karbala, some one hundred miles to the south of Baghdad. The prophet, known to the Arabs and Muslims as the al-Kifil, is mentioned in their Koran and held in great esteem. They believe that he negotiated with the Babylonian king Nebuchadnezzar to spare the captive Jews against a promise of a place in paradise, hence the Arabic name of al-Kifil (the guarantor). That was sometime in the sixth century BC, when the captives were gathered by the King of Kings at a little place called Tal-abib, by the Kebar River, a tributary of the great Euphrates, forty kilometres to the south of Babylon.

The little town of al-Kifil had no connection with the railway system of the country, leaving it accessible only by road or by river in rickety sailing boats or, later on, motorised vessels from Basra in the south. For those travelling from Baghdad or Hilla, their only means of transport was taxis – or lorries, which were far cheaper than the taxis. The Baghdadi taxi drivers hated the prospect of travelling to al-Kifil because of the dusty road, which was a nightmarish succession of holes and humps. During the rainy season, in winter, the road became a long channel of mud littered with marooned vehicles and cursing drivers.

'No, no! You don't have to worry any more,' said Dr Sassoon to one of the taxi drivers. 'Most of the road is now paved with asphalt.'

'No, doctor, I won't go. I tell you even if the road is paved now, not just with asphalt but with lovely white arses and fat pussies all the way from Baghdad to al-Kifil, you won't persuade me to go there.'

Abdul Salam Sassoon had to go with his wife to the Shi'i suburb of Kadhimiah by bus to find a taxi driver willing to leave the easy life of the capital and venture into the dusty south of the country. It was morning and the golden minarets of that jewel of Islamic architecture, the Mosque of Kadhimayn, glittered in the sun. 'Yes, I haven't been to the mosque of al-Kifil. It will be a good opportunity for me to pray to the prophet of the Jews, peace be upon him. Get in and let's go. I'll first fill up with fuel from the petrol station. We won't see another before we arrive in Babylon.'

Karim, the taxi driver, was a man in his thirties, lanky with a narrow upper body and elongated neck like a German wine bottle and as full of gusto. Unlike his colleagues in the job, he enjoyed his work and did everything with a smile, a very rare sight to see in this melancholic country. The colour of his eyes was dark brown, and they were set deep in their sockets. He was not an original inhabitant of Kadhimiah but hailed from the marshland of the deep south, like so many jobbers in this capital who believed that Baghdad's streets were paved with gold and washed with petrol. They threw away their sickles and spades and followed the rural migration to the cities.

The two Sassoons got in with their luggage, and a third person joined them for the journey as far as Saddat al-Hindiyah, the great dam built by the Ottomans over the Euphrates River to bring water to the fields and orange orchards of an area threatened so badly by bouts of famine. The man was a secondary-school teacher going back to his school after a weekend in Baghdad, drinking and whoring. Being a teacher and a fellow traveller, there was no way to stop him talking and asking questions and poor Dr Abdul Salam Sassoon had to endure listening to his lectures and replying to his repeated queries.

'I see you are Jews going to visit the al-Kifil. We also believe in him. He is mentioned in our Koran with Job and Idris as a prophet blessed with the virtue of patience, which you need so desperately in this land, but there is a lot about him in your Torah. He was the one who predicted the return of the Jews to Palestine. The Zionists love him.'

The traveller went silent at this point, regretting bringing up this subject, but he soon recovered to diversify his lecture into a different area. 'Al-Kifil, or, as you call him, Hisqail, is a sacred prophet capable of miracles, incredible miracles. One of my students assured me that the uncle of a friend of his lost his leg in the Iraqi revolution against the British but his wife took him to al-Kifil and, after one night sleeping in his shrine, he woke up in the morning with his leg completely restored and he came out walking. The wife thought that he lost his leg in the first place as a punishment from al-Kifil for taking away his doors during the revolution to use as shields against the British in the war.'

This bald statement was followed by another digression about the link between Judaism and Meso-potamia. 'You know, doctor, our religion is really Arabian and not Iraqi. It came to us from the Arabian Peninsula years ago. And your religion is Iraqi and not Palestinian. You had all your books, your Torah and your Talmud, written here in Babylon. All your prophets are also buried here, your Jonah, your Ezekiel, Daniel, Ezra, Nehemiah and what have you – they are all buried here.'

The driver was getting fed up with all this scholarly talk and determined to put an end to it by

singing. He started with a Niel tune, then he turned
to a Baghdadi *pasta* with a Georgian rhythm:

> You who are digging the well,
> Don't dig too deep with your spade.
> Times may change and you may fall into it.

Like a true Iraqi, the traveller had in turn to butt
in and interrupt the singer.

'That's good, driver. You have a very good voice, I
think you should . . . '

It was now the turn once more of the driver to
interrupt. Encouraged by the approval of the teacher
he began to sing even louder, the homosexual song of
young Hasan:

> Between the shore and the water
> Why did you break my wing, O Hasan?
> Like a duck you shot me, Hasan.
> With your big eyes you killed me.

Dr Sassoon wriggled and kicked. He held his head
with both hands and cried, 'I did not kill her! I did
not kill her. I swear, I did not.' His wife held him
tight, taking him in her arms. 'There, there! It's all
right, it is only a song, you know, my dear. The Song
of Small Hasan – everyone sings it.' She turned to
the driver and whispered, 'Please, no more singing.
My husband is not well. That is why we are taking
him to al-Kifil.' By then, Dr Sassoon was shaking
and sobbing.

It was a relief for her to hear the driver in the end shouting, 'Saddat al-Hindiyah,' and stopping the car to let the teacher out. There were peasant women by the side of the road selling *qaymar*, the famous 'Hindiyah cream', a favourite delicacy. Mrs Sassoon bought a couple of hand-made saucers filled with the cream, as white as toothpaste. It was a God-sent gift with which to pacify Abdul Salam. She filled the freshly baked bread, hot and crispy, with the cream and offered it to her husband. Having emptied them, she added the two crudely made earthenware saucers to their luggage, partly as souvenirs and partly for their rustic attraction. More women were returning from town carrying on their heads stacks of empty wooden containers, having sold their thick yoghurt or *laban* to the townspeople. They spent most of the day travelling, barefoot, some twenty or thirty kilometres, with the full containers balanced precariously but safely on their heads, and then doing the same journey back home with less weight on their heads and more weight in their side pockets. Every day they left their huts at daybreak, with some forty pounds of yoghurt in the wooden utensils, which were kept in place, one on top of the other, by the movement of the women's necks and the swaying of their hips. Like voluptuous belly dancers, they danced their way to town and back, silently and patiently. On Fridays, they came back with tobacco for their men, tea and sugar for the family and, perhaps, some sweets for the kids.

From Saddat al-Hindiyah, the taxi travelled on to Hilla, bypassing the old ruins of Babylon, crossing many canals and rivers, some dry, some full of muddy water which appeared shimmering blue under the clear, azure, cloudless sky. They passed by scattered orchards of fruit trees and palm trees standing together uniformly like soldiers ready for battle. It was harvest time and the bunches of saffron-yellow dates looked like ornaments of gold enticing the passer-by to halt and rob. The driver broke his silence again, but not with singing.

'This land belongs to one of your people, Salih Daniel. He bought it and planted it with all these trees. They call him Abu Sha'ir, the barley man, for filling the area with barley fields and cornfields all the way from Saddat al-Hindiyah. You will see more of him in the town. Some people say that this is Thu Daniel town, not really Thu ul-Kifl.'

Just as he concluded his words, the dome of Ezekiel's mausoleum appeared, rising gradually over the horizon. As the taxi came nearer and nearer to it, this strange example of the typical Mesopotamian tower architecture mixed with Byzantine doming and Islamic motifs found in many other holy locations in Iraq became more defined. The tall structure had plain façades framed and supported by brick columns at its four corners, decorated with the usual geo-metrical Islamic patterns set in the brickwork.

It was nearly lunchtime when the taxicab arrived

100

in al-Kifil and the two passengers invited their driver to join them for a meal of kebab in Suq Daniel, Daniel's market. Mr Salih Daniel was a rich Jewish businessman who was obsessed by the prophet and spent a great deal of money and effort keeping the shrine in good condition. He built this comparatively huge market square of sixty shops over an area of twenty-five hundred square metres with the intention of supporting the upkeep of the shrine with the rent collected from the shopkeepers. The Sassoons were impressed by the aesthetic and architectural features of the suq, which rose to a height of six metres in arches carried by pillared walls. The entrance of the market was adorned on top by the simple shape of the Star of David fixed on a metal plate, but the star had to be removed after the establishment of Israel and the first Arab–Israeli war. It became the symbol of the enemy, what they called the Zionist entity.

The shops were filled with frankincense, jewellery, dates, corn, cloth and farmers' tools. Some shops were occupied by carpenters and tailors. There was, close at hand, one small restaurant providing food, mainly kebabs. To that place the Sassoons took their driver and settled down for lunch. A well-dressed gentleman in Western clothes – a dark suit, clean white shirt and a tasteful tie – stopped and looked at them attentively. He was Mr Ibrahim Moshe Khalaschi, the agent in charge of the Daniel estates, which included this market and all the agricultural lands in the Governorate of Babylon belonging to the Daniels. He could see that this strange couple did not really belong to this or to any other Muslim community. They were not the breast-beating type, wailing for the martyrdom of Imam Hussein. They were more likely Jews of his tribe, he thought, and he stepped forward to bid them good-afternoon, who-ever they might be. His guess was not far off the mark, as he discovered when he spoke to them. In Baghdad Arabic, spoken with a Jewish accent, they introduced themselves and he recognized the name immediately as that of the well-known gynaecologist. Strange, though, Mr Khalaschi thought, for a man of his position and education to take the trouble to come to this place.

'Yes, you can eat the kebabs in this restaurant. This *kebabchi* makes a great effort to ensure that his meat is halal and kosher. He knows that many of his customers may be Jews.'

Mrs Sassoon ventured to satisfy Mr Khalaschi's curiosity by confiding to him that her husband hadn't been feeling well lately and had been advised, by Hakham Eliaho, to complement his medication with the blessings of the prophet Ezekiel.

'Sure! Sure!' said he. 'Hakham Eliaho is a good friend of mine and I'll see that you get all that you seek. Your husband will return a completely different man, with the will of God.'

Mr Khalaschi took them to see the place where

Menahem, the son of the benefactor Salih Daniel, was buried. In another room they saw the simple graves of his sister, his mother and his wife. He finally took them to the tomb of the prophet himself, the climax of the visit. It was like the shrine of any Muslim saint but, of course, inscribed with Hebrew as well as Arabic. There was a great deal of fussy embellishment on every side, with abstract figures and botanic motifs representing the afterlife. The abstract decoration was carried on over the tiled floor in the geometric patterns. Above the Hebrew panelling, which rose some three or four metres high on every wall, there were small windows allowing light to shine over the tomb, which was covered with a heavy embroidered cloth. Generations of Jews, Christians and Muslims had stood and prayed in front of it with awe and veneration. Dr Abdul Salam Sassoon, atheist as he was, could not help feeling overwhelmed by the atmosphere of the place. He was looking down, lost in contemplation, when he felt a hand touching him on his right shoulder. It wasn't Ezekiel's hand but that of Shammash Menashi, the high priest of the shrine. As Dr Sassoon turned his face towards him, the shammash handed him a little booklet with a certain page open for him to read. It was the collection of prayers penned by Ben Ish Hai especially for this holy place. Dr Sassoon looked at the words and his lips seemed to murmur something.

It was time to vacate the place for Muslims to

come in and do their own evening prayers. Dressed in his traditional kaftan and wearing a red fez wrapped with a *chitaya* cloth on his head, Shammash Menashi led the couple into another room where he welcomed them warmly and chatted with them casually.

'If only I could sleep,' Dr Sassoon lamented. 'It is this problem of sleep which is so unsettling, so worrying. I panic. Every time I put my head on the pillow, I worry that I won't be able to sleep. Then I panic because I am afraid I won't sleep. When I do sleep, as soon as I drop off I get these terrible dreams, these nightmares, nightmares of blood and monsters. I wake up terrified and again I panic.'

'You won't have any more of these nightmares with the blessing of Ezekiel. Worse cases have come here and have been cured.'

'I panic. I panic that I won't sleep and I panic when I do sleep and the panic wakes me up. I get up and go for a walk. But as soon as I start walking, I get tired and feel the desire to go back to my bed.'

'Ezekiel will sort you out.' The shammash put his hand gently on Abdul Salam's head and started to mumble, in Hebrew, verses from the Song of Songs. The doctor had his eyes closed, trying to pick up what it was the man was reciting.

'Ezekiel will give you peace and cure you. You will sleep in his arms. You will sleep here. When these Muslims finish their prayers they will go and leave the place to Beni Israel. Did you bring blankets with you?'

'No, we didn't think of it.'

'The shops are still open. Go and buy yourselves a couple of blankets. You will sleep by the side of the tomb. Spread one blanket underneath and cover yourself with another and put your head on the divine stone I shall indicate to you. Lie there the whole night with your head on the stone.'

The shammash then prescribed for him verses from the Torah to recite a hundred times. Not so sure that her husband would do the reciting, Tiffaha Sassoon volunteered to do it for him. All her life she had been doing things for him. Why not recite the Torah for him as well?

'We leave the light on all the time. The place is full of snakes and scorpions, all sorts of insects. You keep a good watch,' Shammash Menashi whispered to Mrs Sassoon.

'Ooh! Don't tell him that.'

'No. But just keep a good watch. Stamp on them with your shoes and kill them. The whole country is full of snakes and scorpions. Good-night.'

Dr Abdul Salam Sassoon folded his blanket and spread it on the tiled floor and stretched out as directed. Tiffaha covered him with the other blanket and sat by his side, fully awake throughout the night, reciting the text given to her. Strange, she thought, to hear him snoring in a place of stone like this, surrounded by snakes and scorpions, and not in his own comfortable bed back at home! As the minutes ticked by, a few more people joined them, some with sick children. Touching the tomb with their hands, they prayed in Arabic, Hebrew and Judeo-Arabic and must have kept the prophet fully occupied with all their diverse requests. One woman sat in a remote corner, her child in her lap feeding from her shrivelled breast, and sobbed quietly. A man approached her and asked her in a harsh voice to keep quiet or else get out. With nothing else to do other than recite the prescribed scripture, Tiffaha Sassoon drifted in her mind from one thought to another. She remembered all the men she had loved and all those who had loved her, like Sami Shaul who wanted to marry her and take her to America. Why did she say no? It is not easy to be a Jew and a woman in Iraq. Will things settle down or will they, the Arabs and Jews, fight it out to the bitter end in Palestine. It will be a tough time for the Jews in Baghdad.

She remembered Abbas Baizah, the lunatic who wandered around the bazaars and public places in the city followed by crowds of urchins ridiculing him and throwing stones at him. Every time he was hit by a stone thrown from behind him, he would pick it up and throw it at whoever was in front of him. The urchins would roar with laughter and the injured man would turn and give Abbas Baizah a frightful beating. The fool would then scream and cry in pain. More laughter and merriment from the kids. Tiffaha saw the spectacle more than once in al-Samaw'al Street and it stuck in her mind. Isn't it just like the story of the Jews in the Arab world? Whenever the Arabs are beaten by the Israeli forces in Palestine, they take it out on their own Jews and attack their shops and houses. It is Abbas Baizah's story on a larger scale. Tiffaha went round and round in her recollections and her thoughts. Why does Abdul Salam keep saying, 'I didn't kill her?' Who is she – the woman he killed or didn't kill? Why does he keep repeating it, over and over? Should I ask him? Should I try to find out? What if I discover that he did actually kill someone? Perhaps a Muslim woman? Someone he loved? Could it be that he has been unfaithful to me? All this anxious feminine speculation was played out against the night-long croaking of frogs, flirting or having discussions by the banks of the Kebar River near by. Their hollow voices were drowned, from time to time, by the baleful howling of angry dogs furiously swearing at each other in the various villages and barley fields far away. Zooming and zizzing, the flies, mosquitoes and other creatures of the air kept on buzzing in Tiffaha's milky ears, hopping on to her delicate face and biting her bare arms. Quivering with frustration, she waved them away or swatted them, wondering if they ever slept. How is it that flies don't need to sleep? Do they also suffer from insomnia and so go out to torment the people around them?

Tiffaha's train of thought was finally interrupted by the voice of the muezzin, intoning his call to the dawn prayer from the solitary minaret of this religious compound. 'Allahu akbar. Allahu akbar!' The Muslims in the shrine echoed his words softly. Some got up and went out to do their ablutions in preparation for prayer. No sooner did they finish with that sacred task than the early morning sunlight penetrated the simple mausoleum from the square eastern window and made all the brick decorations appear bold and compelling. Some of the sun's golden rays fell on the tomb's textiles in such a way as to make oblong shapes which looked like giant yellow banknotes.

The whole place was quite different in the morning. A pack of hungry mongrels, misshapen and rough, with legs like dry sticks, stood at the entrance and looked to see if anyone had started to eat or if their sense of smell had deceived them. They were soon joined by beggars looking for alms. 'Give us some of what God has given you, for the sake of him, God's prophet, al-Kifil.' The dogs did not like their appearance or their words and barked at them as a way of saying, in canine language, 'I don't approve of you or of what you are saying. Buzz off or we'll bite you.' Their voices, however, sounded hoarse and tired, probably on account of all the howling they had done during the night. The beggars took no notice of them. They were used to being snarled at and shooed away. But the barking woke up the doctor who rubbed his eyes and looked around. To his surprise, the first face he saw was that of his taxi driver who had crept in during the night and slept opposite the Sassoons.

'Oh, you are here! What brought you here?'

'I also have something I want Prophet al-Kifil, peace be upon him, to help me with.'

'What is it, Karim?'

'I want al-Kifil to find me a good wife, a woman who can read and write. I am fed up with being unable to write. Every time I have to get something written I have to go and pay some *ardhahalchi* to write it for me. I want a woman who can write.'

'I don't think you will find one here. But be careful, Ezekiel is a Jew. He may give you a Jewish woman.'

'Oh, that will be good. A Yahudiah makes a good mother and a good wife. Good in bed. Why not? The Prophet Muhammad had a Jewish wife, Safiah.'

The words amused the doctor and made him laugh heartily, and it cheered up Tiffaha to see her husband laughing again. Ezekiel's medicine seemed to have worked. Even the doctor thought so.

'I think I am feeling better. I had quite a good night,' Dr Sassoon declared. He looked tired but truly cheerful. They walked to the same kebab shop and ordered a breakfast of buffalo cream and date syrup, *dibis*, which was immediately brought to them, with *istikans* of strong black tea and hot bread in the shape of large discs, twice the size of the old 33rpm gramophone records and as reliable. Other customers in the kebab restaurant, in their *abayas* and *dishdashas*, white for men and black for women, could not help feeling curious as to the identity of these three characters. Sensing their gaze, Tiffaha turned to the driver and whispered in his ear, 'Please, Karim, don't tell them that my husband is Abdul Salam Sassoon, the gynaecologist. We'll have all the women of Babylon crowding around us. They will stop praying to al-Kifil and hassle my husband to give them babies.'

Poor Ezekiel, what a burden he had had to carry for two thousand five hundred years, striving to sort out the prayers of those who wanted babies and of the others who didn't want to get pregnant, and making sure he didn't get them mixed up. But then, he was the steward of King Nebuchadnezzar, and good stewards never get their orders mixed up. That was the secret of keeping the population of Mesopotamia under control.

Abdul Salam Sassoon settled the *kebabchi*'s bill and went back to the shrine, where he saw a number of sheep, all certified kosher for a thanksgiving sacrifice to the prophet and subsequent distribution to the poor. The doctor gave two dinars for one of the best available animals and turned away.

'Have you seen the animal slaughtered and apportioned?' Mr Khalaschi asked as he met the Sassoons leaving the shrine.

'Oh, no.'

'Well then, the man will sell the same animal to the next visitor. That was not very clever,' chuckled the agent.

'What does it matter. It will be alms given to a deserving shepherd. He is just as poor.'

The Sassoons thanked him for all he had done for them and invited him to visit them next time he was in Baghdad. 'By all means, I'll do so. But you must also come here again. Make it on the Ziarah Day. People will be pouring in from Baghdad, Basra and other parts of the country. There will be a lot of chanting and fun.'

The couple gave him their promise again, shook hands with him and bade him farewell. The taxi was waiting for them. 'Which way do you want to go now?' asked Karim, the driver. 'To ancient Babylon? It would be my chance to see the place, if you don't mind. It's only a small detour from the route to Baghdad.'

The doctor readily agreed and Tiffaha was pleased to notice the change in her husband's mood. He was himself again, taking an interest in things. Like most of the Iraqi educated élite, he was acquainted with the ancient history of the country, and especially Babylon because of its close association with the whole history of Iraqi Jewry and the development of Judaism. It took the driver half an hour to reach the small car park on the outskirts of the old city, the metropolis of the ancient world and centre of civilization, now reduced to a series of dusty mounds of earth and rubble. On the highest spot stood the famous Lion of Babylon, straddling a low plinth of cement and bricks of a more recent date. The huge granite lion with its massive head represented the chief goddess, Ishtar. There was a woman of granite lying beneath it. Abdul Salam Sassoon stood and gazed at this peculiar composition of a lion bestride a submissive woman. Was it savagery vanquishing civilization? Could be. This would be just like the history of Mesopotamia. Maybe it was something else. Power protecting the nation against the alien invaders. Another view of the country's history. But this is in fact supposed to be the goddess Ishtar standing over her mother; Ishtar, the forerunner of Venus and the Virgin Mary, the giver of life with no male partner. She is the symbol of Mesopotamia's early recognition of the power of feminism. Ishtar defending the land and its citizenry. Ishtar Sassoon, the defender of her little citizen, picked up her camera and took a snapshot of Ishtar Babylon before moving on, with Salam, to make the customary walk along the processional street of the ancient city, the Pall Mall of Babylon. This early prototype of a boulevard led to the Gate of Ishtar and the Royal Palace of King Nebuchadnezzar, emperor and conqueror of Jerusalem. Along both sides of the street they saw the glazed bas-reliefs of Mesopotamian wild and domestic animals. How did they come to disappear from this part of the world? There were no more lions or leopards or similar wild animals left

in modern-day Iraq. What had happened to them?
How did this magnificent animal, the lion, head of the
animal kingdom, disappear from the land without any
trace other than these bas-reliefs and the far-fetched
tales told by the old to their grandchildren or by the
eloquent storytellers to their amazed listeners in the
traditional coffee houses. So many kings ruled and
disappeared, toppled, slain and dragged through the
streets of these ancient towns. Like so many other
creatures of land, water and air, wild cats, peaceful
birds and tiny insects, they lived, hunted, perished
and disappeared, some leaving just a faint record and
some without any trace.

It was nearly evening when Karim sat in front of
his driving wheel and revved his engine. The sun, red
and spectacular like an ancient god, was going
down behind a layer of blue smoke rising from the
hundreds of *tannurs*, the old circular baking ovens. It
was time for the womenfolk to bake bread, *khubz* and
khubz uruq, with minced meat, parsley and onions,
for their exhausted men coming back from the fields
of wheat and barley. The smell of the bread mixed
appetizingly with the blue smoke of the burning cow-
dung and turf, the customary fuel for the *tannurs*.
Sturdy, tattooed women in black *futas* and navy-blue
dishdashas stood with long wooden poles to poke the
fire and keep it under control, sweating and swearing
at their children all the time. Groups of fellaheen, with
their ancient spades and axes on their shoulders,

were walking home, chatting, coughing, laughing and singing the sad *abudia* songs along the way. Here and there was a solitary fellah who preferred to walk apart, brooding with downcast eyes and talking to himself, for even among the peasant community there was always the individualist, the lonely figure who kept aloof, buried in his own thoughts. They were all fellaheen working for Salih Abu Sha'ir, Salih Daniel, the benevolent Jewish landowner, coming back from his barley fields in this fertile province of Babylon, fed by the Euphrates River and its numerous irrigation canals. The western wind was pursuing its perennial task of blowing gently from the great Syrian desert, without ever succeeding in carrying away in its folds the lazy *tannur* smoke which preferred to hang over the little mud houses and humble straw huts of the village. Through the layers of the smoke, the cooing of the pigeons could be heard as they roosted in the branches of the citrus trees. Their low-pitched voices were occasionally drowned by the croaking sound of the ravens.

'Ibqi'! Ibqi'!' Tiffaha snarled at them.

'You Jews don't like ravens, do you?' remarked the driver.

'They are horrible. You shouldn't like them either. They are an ill omen.'

At Saddat al-Hindiyah, Tiffaha stopped the car to buy some of the Hindiyah buffalo cream as presents for friends, especially for Hakham Eliaho. 'They are pretty women, these *qaymar* women,' she teased Karim, the driver. 'Why don't you pick one of them for a wife? Look at that pretty one with the beauty spots tattooed on her cheek and chin. Look how she is swaying with her hips!'

'Oh, madam, what are you saying? Marry one of these harlots who sleep with any drunken lorry driver for a dirham?'

'Come on, Karim. Don't be mean and say such things.'

'I want to marry a woman who can read and write, I told you. What would I do with these ignorant buffalo women?'

'I can tell you, Karim, many of my rich patients look like buffaloes,' quipped Dr Sassoon.

Karim loaded the Hindiyah cream bowls into the car boot, covering them carefully and making sure that they wouldn't turn over and add their contents to the grease and engine oil. They all resumed their seats and continued their journey, passing by the Musayyab Bridge on their left then pressing on through the small town of Mahmudiah and the agricultural village of Alexandria until they reached the tiny village of Latifiah. The traffic was suddenly heavy, moving in stops and starts and coming eventually to a complete halt. They were getting near to Baghdad, it was true, but the driver said that he had never experienced such a delay. Passengers and drivers started to climb out of their vehicles to get some fresh air and exercise.

'What is happening here?'

'It could be a *coup d'état*, who knows? The whole country is restive. They believe the armed forces are not doing enough for the Palestinians. They are not helping them.'

'No, no. All the army generals are faithful to the king and his regent. They are carefully selected. They will never rise against him.'

'Ha! Ha! Don't you believe, my friend, in the loyalty of a soldier.'

Groups of people gathered around, feeling fed up, talking and demanding to know what was happening. When would the traffic ever move? Is it a serious accident? So many cars stationery and scattered over the narrow road. Maybe it is a camel or a cow run over by a lorry. Where are the police? They are never where they are wanted. Probably they are too busy dividing the profits with the pickpockets and street walkers. Anyway, can someone call them?

A bicycle was spotted on the other side, travelling in the opposite direction, loaded with onions and lettuces.

'Hey, my young lad, do you know why the traffic is not moving?' shouted one of the drivers to the cyclist.

'The army. Army convoy moving.'

'Oh, didn't I tell you?' said a man to his companion in response. 'Whenever something is wrong, it is the army doing something. It is always the same story.'

There was nothing to be done but sit and wait. Women started to unpack food and offer sandwiches to their young ones. The men occupied themselves by rolling cigarettes and smoking. Those who could salvage some old newspaper began to read whatever story they managed to find. The drivers occupied themselves by attending to their neglected engines. A few old men went a short distance away, spread out their *abayas* in the direction of Mecca and started to do their evening prayers. But this holy duty was soon cut short as the traffic started to move. They hurriedly slipped their feet into their sandals, picked up their *abayas* and started to run behind their trucks or buses, shouting and swearing. Everyone rushed back to his place, praising Allah and thanking his prophets, but after one or two hundred metres everything came to a halt again. Another half an hour passed and they were once more on the move. But as they came closer to where the road leading to Falluja crossed the highway to Jordan, they began to hear a distant clamour of people chanting. The voices became clearer although mixed with the roar of heavy vehicles.

'Long live the Iraqi army!'
'Long live Arab Palestine!'
'Down with Israel.'
'Down with Zionism.'

There were crowds of students and young people, men and women, shouting slogans and cheering the

Iraqi army as its military hardware of troop carriers,
loaded with soldiers festooned with rifles and equipment, tank carriers, supply lorries, artillery pieces,
drawn by their field carriages, Red Crescent ambu-
lances and vehicles of all kinds and shapes in their
camouflage colours roared by. They were all on their
way to Jordan and then Palestine to join other Arab
armies in overthrowing the state of Israel.

The crowd of young students was feeling elated
and encouraged by the strength of the convoy and the
sight of the men waving their hands and clenching
their fists in a gesture of resolve. The students waved
back and cheered them on.

'Death to Zionism!'

'Death to the Jews!'

'Death to all Jews!'

Dr Abdul Salam Sassoon began to feel claustro-
phobic inside the taxi. He started sweating, his heart
began beating like a loud oven clock, his chest was
getting tight and his breathing was becoming short
and hard.

'Death to all Jews . . . '

'Death to all Jews . . . '

' . . . to all Jews.'

Abdul Salam Sassoon put his fingers in his ears in
a vain attempt to stop the noise. The taxicab was
moving slowly but he opened the door, gritted his
teeth and jumped out, falling on his face. He
staggered to his feet and started in the opposite

direction, away from the chanting crowds and back towards al-Kifil. Karim stopped his car, leapt out, and with Tiffaha, ran after him, ignoring the cars behind, whose drivers began to hoot and bellow. Between the two of them, they managed to hold the doctor and gently persuade him back to his place in the taxi. He was shaking, writhing and sweating. His face was pale, his eyes blotchy and his lips were dry like the skin of a shrimp.

Tiffaha put her slender right arm around him and with her other hand took a lace handkerchief from her handbag to wipe the blood from his grazed nose. Abdul Salam Sassoon did not have the distinctive Semitic nose, beloved of anti-Semitic cartoonists. But his smaller nose was no advantage in his facial collision with mother earth, from which mother earth emerged intact but he suffered a damaged bridge. Tiffaha wiped it and cared for it as much as she could. With soft words and softer touches, she managed to calm Abdul Salam's tormented breast and bring him back to some semblance of normality. 'I am sorry for all this,' he murmured in the direction of the driver.

By then, they had managed to cover a couple of kilometres more, reaching Jisr al-Khir. The noisy youth were far behind and their clamour was only a faint hubbub far away. Karim had to stop his taxi once more at a road junction to allow another military contingent to pass. Abdul Salam was too tired this time to take much notice of the passing troop carriers. Had he

been more alert he would probably have spotted a
face not altogether unfamiliar to him. It is true that
when soldiers are dressed in their uniforms with their
helmets on, it becomes very difficult to differentiate
between them. They all look alike. But this particular
one stood out because he was not wearing a helmet,
suggesting he had a rather rebellious spirit which
army discipline had not managed to suppress. At
least, not for the time being. As this young soldier,
tall and broad in the chest, had his helmet pushed
back, he revealed a handsome face with beautiful
hazel eyes and curly dark hair. Had Dr Sassoon
managed to take more interest in the occupants of
these troop carriers, he would probably have recognized the face of the young fellow who had called at
his surgery and questioned him about the fate of a
certain young lady of the name of Samira Haj Nufal
al-Mumduh. But Abdul Salam Sassoon didn't pay
much attention to the troopers and the young soldier
passed him unnoticed. Indeed, the same thing could
be said about the soldier, Private Hassun Abd al-Ali.
For had he paid more attention to the occupants
of this particular taxicab, he would have recognized
the same gynaecologist whom he had called on and
then lost touch with. The very man he wanted to see
again. But both passed each other like two ships in
the ocean. Dr Abdul Salam Sassoon was on his way
back to his surgery and Private Hassun Abd al-Ali
was marching, so to speak, to war.

⚜ 10 ⚜

Rendezvous with Karim

Friends and fellow members of the Baghdadi Jewish community were more than relieved to see Abdul Salam Sassoon back in circulation and attending to his professional duties. They showered him with calls of congratulation and invitations to dinner parties, wedding celebrations, bar mitzvah functions and all kinds of clubbing and evenings out.

Moshe Na'im, a cloth importer and property owner, hosted a lavish *masquf* party at his *chardagh*, one of those large huts of wooden poles, straw mats and straw screens that the Baghdadis construct temporarily for the summer as houses of fun on the sandy beaches of the Tigris River. A dozen expensive *shabbut* fish were cleaned, sprinkled with spices and covered with tomato slices and onion rings, grilled on the open wood fire and served with mango pickle and round, crispy bread. They were washed down with the traditional drinks of arak and Diana beer to the accompaniment of songs and music from the wind-up HMV gramophone. Abdul Salam Sassoon brought with him his oud and started to play 'Wish That I Had Wings' and various other compositions by Sharif Muhiddeen, but as Sattuta, one of the guests who was known to have an agreeable voice, joined him, he retuned his oud to accompany her in singing some of Salima Murad's best loved songs.

> *Malyan Kul gulbi hachi,*
> *Ilman agulan wa ashtachi?*
> *Ma yinf'a 'glaibi al-Nadam,*
> *Ma tishba' ayvri bachi.*

> My heart is full of words,
> To whom can I speak and moan?
> Regret will not help my little heart,
> My eyes do not cry enough.

Sattuta went on and on, moving from Salima Murad's songs to favourites by Um Kalthum and Afifa Iskander, until her husband signalled her to stop, sensing that the others had had enough and wanted to talk, for singing and music in the Arab world should only be treated as an interlude or serve as a background to conversation, the real passion of the Middle East. This art of enjoying words has become limited in more recent times to the obsessive discussion of politics. Abdul Salam Sassoon put his instrument back in its case and Sattuta moved over to help herself to more pieces of the *masquf* fish.

'I heard from a very reliable source, the nephew of a typist in the Ministry of Social Affairs, that the government intends to expel all Jews to Israel,' said Salim Abdul Nabi, but his friend, Dr Akram Alim, contradicted him. 'No, Salim. I told you many times not to believe this gossip. The Arabs want to keep their Jews as a surety and a good source of money. They will only get rid of them when Abu Naji tells them to do so.'

Everybody believed that all their affairs were run from London and nothing could be done without orders from Whitehall. Hamid Qadri, one of the few Muslims in this gathering and a member of the National Democratic Party, chipped in: 'The Arabs are stupid in persecuting the Jews. They are doing the dirty work for the Zionists. That is what the Zionists want. Put pressure on the Jews and make them go to Israel and rally round the Jewish state as their only protector. Jews have lived amonge us for centuries. No one bothered them before.'

'Come now, Abu Qahtan, don't exaggerate. Yes, we tolerated them, but only as second-class citizens.'

'But they were better off here than they were in Europe.'

'Sure, sure. No question of that.'

The discussion then turned to the subject of the latest arrests, the Communists who were arrested for being Jews and the Jews who were arrested for being Communists. There was the subject of sureties and the latest amounts the Jews had to pay as an indemnity against the chance of their spying for Israel.

'Poor Hisqail! He had to marry his ugly cousin who

paid the five thousand dinars to the court and got him out.'

'Yes, I saw him last week. Do you know what he said to me? I asked him, "How are things with you, Hisqail?" He said, "Worse than being a Shi'i in Saudi Arabia. I got myself out of one prison and went into another." Poor fellow. Such a fine artist he is.'

Abdul Salam, tiring of all this sour conversation, took off his shirt and dived into the water. Tiffaha joined him and both swam to the middle of the river and back. He threw himself on a bed of sand, warm like the bosom of a well-rounded woman. He lay on his stomach for a couple of minutes listening to the music carried by the fresh west wind from the other *chardaghs* scattered all along the sandy beach. He turned on his back and gazed up at the dark sky filled with stars glittering like distant fireworks, millions of miles away, so far yet seeming so near. Is it more beautiful, Abdul Salam asked himself, to see the stars shining more brightly when there is no moon, or to see the moon at her most brilliant, outshining all the stars?

'Time to go home, darling,' Tiffaha sang.

When Abdul Salam picked himself up he found most of the others already gone, but the stars remained glittering silently over the noisy city.

Victoria was excited to hear the familiar footsteps of Dr Sassoon coming up the stairs after such a long absence. A mountain of letters, medical reports and invitations to international conferences had piled up on his desk and the torrent of enquiries from patients, old and new, to which his secretary had not known how to reply, had never stopped. 'Wonderful! Wonderful!' she breathed, unable to resist hugging her boss and planting a warm kiss on his cheek. 'So good to see you back. I knew you would be back. I knew it.'

The pharmacist felt equally relieved to see Abdul Salam's Oldsmobile pulling into the same old spot and the doctor emerging from it. 'Welcome back, Dr Abdul Salam.'

The butcher, however, was not so pleased to see the doctor, fearing he would resume his old habit of advising people not to eat meat.

The homecoming joys and celebrations, sadly, were short lived, for as Abdul Salam Sassoon opened his letters he found one from the Faculty of Medicine informing him that his lectures at the faculty were no longer needed. A few days later a similar letter reached him from the Royal Hospital's antenatal department, with similar expressions of regret. His medical practice was confined to the private work he carried out in his surgery. His patients, however, dwindled in number as they heard of his dismissal and the government's suspicion of him. More patients drifted away as his work once more began to suffer on account of his recurring mental problems. Rumours circulated that he had fled the country to Iran. Others said that he had been arrested for espionage and would soon be put on trial in the military court. Some people believed that he had been killed for seducing a Muslim woman, one of his patients, the wife of a cabinet minister. Even his old patients stopped calling at his surgery for it was unwise for a woman to entrust her womb to a Jew. Yet Dr Sassoon had to go on paying his secretary and meet all the bills of his clinic.

Tiffaha was reduced to half her weight by worry about her husband's mental state. His appearance and his behaviour were deteriorating from day to day, and he had gone back to repeating his old refrain, 'I didn't kill her, I didn't,' hysterically whenever he heard the front doorbell. Just for being reminded by his wife one morning to brush his teeth, he broke the toothbrush violently in pieces and threw them in her face. Next thing, she thought, he will break my teeth in another fit of temper for not buying him a new toothbrush! Something more had to be done other than doling out those useless tablets and vitamin pills and hoping for the best. Another visit to Hakham Eliaho would not go amiss.

The old synagogue had its gate firmly locked and it took her some five minutes of knocking to elicit a response in the form of the curtain of a small window on the first floor being drawn slightly back to allow somebody to inspect the caller. It was another five minutes before she heard a muffled voice behind the door calling, 'Who is it?'

'I am Tiffaha Sassoon.'

'What do you want?'

'I want to see Hakham Ekiaho.'

It was yet another five minutes before somebody inserted a key in the ancient lock and opened the door hesitantly, like a cat trying a new recipe. 'Come in then.' She went in and the door was immediately shut and double-locked behind her. The rabbi was not sitting on his usual wooden *takhat* in the open courtyard. An old woman with a hunched back and supported by a walking stick beckoned to the visitor with a shaking hand to follow her. She was led to a small and dark inner room, lit with a bare light bulb hanging from the ceiling and lined with old cupboards full of leather-bound books. The cupboards were heavily stacked on top with newspapers, magazines and thick files. The air smelt rancid and patches of damp were causing the old paint to crack and fall, exposing the rough brick and plasterwork. The crumbling plaster fell to the floor and mixed with the old dust, affording a ready home for ants and other tiny insects.

The rabbi was sitting on a cane chair made more comfortable with the help of two cushions, one for the seat and one for the back. In front of this rough old chair, a remnant of the First World War, stood a square wooden table on which were spread bundles of documents and papers the old man in the kaftan was studying. He took off his reading glasses with gold rims and got up to welcome the familiar visitor. 'Ahlan, ahlan, my daughter.' He pulled another cane chair for her and invited her to sit down.

'Yes, I have heard a lot about your husband lately. I am sorry that he has not improved. Nothing seemed to help him. His trouble is that he is a very sensitive character. Now, what are you going to do about him?'

'This is what I have come about. What do you advise me to do, Hakham Eliaho?'

'Doctora, listen to me. This is no place for your husband to recover his wits. Things are driving us all round the bend. The whole country has gone mad. Have you heard of the artist, Na'im Abdul Aziz? He is just a painter, a graduate of the Fine Arts Institute. They accused him of spying for Israel and put him in gaol. I wouldn't be surprised at all if they put Dr Sassoon in prison as well. Take him out of the country before they do.'

'Yes, I thought of that. But how can we leave Iraq? They won't give us passports.'

Hakham Eliaho scraped the floor with his cane chair, and pulling a few inches closer to her, bent over towards her and whispered: 'Do what other Jews are doing. With a few dinars, get somebody to smuggle you out to Iran. From there, you can go anywhere you want. The Shah of Iran is keeping his eyes shut.'

Having said that, the old man drew back and,

stroking his white silky beard, waited for her response.

'No. You need a man with all his wits to do that. Abdul Salam is in no shape for a brush with the border police. The moment they question him, he will simply repeat, "I didn't kill her." '

Deadlock! There was a pause of silence lasting a few seconds with each interlocutor fixing the other with thoughtful eyes. The rabbi bent forward again, even closer to her this time, and broke the silence with a hiss. 'My daughter, listen carefully and do not impart anything of what I am going to tell you. This is very confidential information. I heard from my own reliable sources that the government is about to issue a new law allowing all Jews to emigrate to Israel. They are getting as fed up with us as we are with them. They will freeze all our properties. The clever ones should sell as soon as possible before registering for emigration. Do you follow what I am telling you?'

Tiffaha nodded her head and rose to leave, without adding a word to the conversation other than wishing the rabbi good health and bidding him goodbye. He walked with her to the door of the synagogue, turned the key and opened it for her. They exchanged meaningful looks and these were enough.

A few more days and Hakham Eliaho's words became a reality. The nationality-cancellation law was promulgated hastily and Jews rushed to apply for emigration. They had at first applied in dribs and drabs as they regarded the measure with typical Middle Eastern suspicion. But emigration registration soon gathered momentum and became a stampede when bombs were thrown at some Jewish gatherings. Israel accused the Muslims of terrorizing the Jews and the government accused Israel of sending agents to create panic and cause the Jews to leave the country. The airlines hired for transporting the emigrants had to remove the usual passenger seats to make more room for the emigrants and pack them in like sheep and cattle. But the people were quite satisfied. Leaving the country, although with tears and heartfelt sobbing, was all that mattered. It was only one hour's flight to Israel. The children were screaming with excitement, the old crying and reciting prayers, the women grasping the arms of their menfolk tightly. All in all, there had been nothing like it in the whole history of the Jewish race and Judaism, perhaps with the exception of the expulsion of Jews from England and Andalusia during the Middle Ages.

'It is written,' said an old man with a long beard and balding head, just like the image of a biblical prophet in a children's book. 'God shall bring the Israelites back to Zion. They shall soar on the wings of eagles. That is what these aeroplanes are. It is the prophecy fulfilled.'

As soon as they squatted on the floor and the

airliner roared and took off, with the passengers grasping each other from fear and anxiety, the old man led them in religious chants. 'For it is also written: They will enter Zion singing.' Back in the Jewish district, Aqd al-Yahud, a few vulnerable souls could not take the strain and committed suicide, leaving their families, whose turn it was to take their place in the airliners, with the tragic task of having to bury a loved one in a sinner's grave in a hurry.

Amid the turmoil of Operation Ezra and Nehemiah, the name given by the people involved to the exodus of the Iraqi Jews, negative news began to filter out from Israel to the community in Baghdad that the new arrivals had found nothing like the milk and honey promised to them. The Sassoons hesitated to turn their backs on the country in which they had been born and brought up to join the struggle to bring about this 'free homeland and happy nation'; to abandon the graves of their fathers and forefathers and to embark on a new life amidst people with whom they had nothing in common other than the religion for which they didn't care. Time passed. They suddenly found themselves stuck with their old country as the deadline for taking the option of emigration to Israel stipulated by the law was reached. When Tiffaha had finally managed to persuade her husband to give up everything and go, she found it was too late. As most of the other Sassoons, kinsmen and friends, had already 'caught

the wings of the eagles' and gone, life in Baghdad
became even more oppressive, lonely and precarious
for those left behind. They just had to take the plunge,
sell everything, shut up shop and find a way out.

Tiffaha had often had occasion over the years to
put on the black *abaya* and masquerade as a Muslim
woman. Her past experiences came in handy at this
delicate point in time. She didn't need to go far as she
had, in her own house, a couple of these *abaya* cloaks
which she often wore when visiting the strict Muslim
districts of Baghdad, like the Karkh area, and sometimes for the occasional fancy-dress party at the
Ilwiyah Club in the better days of Iraq's contemporary history. She took these two *abayas* out of
the cupboard, shook them, ironed them and selected
one for this new venture which she had never
expected to have to undertake. After dressing herself
modestly, Tiffaha enveloped herself in the *abaya* and
walked about in the house for a few moments of
practice. This done, she picked up her handbag and
left home without breathing a word to her husband
about her immediate mission.

'See you soon, darling. I wont be long,' she called
to him and dashed out without giving him time to ask
her where she was going.

Iraq is said to be a land of extremes, a reputation
which seems to be well earned even by its rivers.
There is a considerable difference in the level of water
between springtime, when the snow starts melting in

the high mountains of Turkey, Kurdistan and Iran, the source of the Mesopotamian rivers, and summer-time, when there is no more snow to melt or clouds in the heavens to rain. During the *sayhud*, the low-level period, the pontoon bridge of Kadhimiah dropped quite a few metres from the street and bridge-head level, which made it immensely difficult for the horse-drawn carriages to ascend and even more difficult to descend. As so often happened, a single donkey pulling a heavily loaded wagon could not make it and collapsed in the middle of the narrow bridge, turning its rickety wagon on its side and shedding the cargo of tomatoes all over the place. The traffic was brought to a halt. In their anger and frustration, the car drivers hooted and shouted at the wagon man.

'What do you expect me to do? Don't you see the Almighty Allah collapsed on his knees here?' answered the wagon man pointing to the donkey. He would give no way to any traffic before collecting his tomatoes, repacking his boxes, reloading his wagon and persuading his exhausted beast to accept meekly the woes of life in Iraq and make another attempt at the uphill ascent.

Unwilling to wait for this rigmarole to be con-cluded, Mrs Sassoon paid her taxi driver and decided to meet the challenge and ascend the bridge herself on foot. She made it and went on to complete the remaining part of the journey to the Kadhimayn Mosque under her own steam. It was an hour's walk and she was exposed all the way to the burning August sun and the curious and suspicious gaze of onlookers. She did not look like a local woman and her gait under the *abaya* was not quite right somehow. Who was she and what was she up to in those troubled times? They followed her with their inquisitive eyes, but luckily for Mrs Sassoon they did not challenge her. Tired, sweating and covered with holy dust, the Jewish lady arrived safely at the taxi rank outside the Golden Mosque and the bazaar which surrounded it. She adjusted the *abaya* to allow herself a small chink for observation, but she couldn't find the object of her hazardous quest. Karim, the taxi driver, was not there. She decided to wait. Maybe he would soon turn up.

Her patience and tactics paid dividends in the end, but just as she caught sight of his taxi and was about to approach him, other women, with their children and their shopping, got in before her and made themselves comfortable on the back seat. Tiffaha, however, managed to make herself known to Karim, who arranged to pick her up on his next round. This meant roughly another hour of waiting and she decided to spend the time visiting the bazaar. The aroma of the famous Kadhimiah kebabs drew her to the meat market where she saw, for the first time in her life, a camel-meat butcher's shop, recognizable from the grotesque head of that strange desert animal, the ship of the Sahara, with its sarcastic grin, protruding yellow teeth and long neck, nailed on top of the ramshackle establishment, looking firm and mighty like the barrel of a heavy gun melted and twisted by the heat of fire. Next door, there was a simple tailor of dwarfish stature measuring up a Bedouin from the Jazira wasteland in the west for a white *dishdasha*. Groups of sunburnt dairy maids, with cheeks and chins tattooed in blue, were squatting on the asphalt pavement, feeding their famished babies and selling their produce of butter, cream and yoghurt. Beginning to feel thirsty, she purchased a glass of iced pomegranate juice, which was so sweet, red and refreshing it tempted her to buy a whole basket of the nourishing fruit. She felt duty bound not to deprive her husband of this seasonal delicacy.

The avenue of shops and street peddlers led Tiffaha, in the end, to the steps of the great mausoleum of Imam Musa al-Kadhim, another descendant of the Prophet Muhammad. The lavish splendour of the mosque was in complete contrast to what the Jewish lady was used to seeing in the bare simplicity of the great synagogue in Aqd al-Yahud. She was overwhelmed by the inventiveness of the shrine's design, its silhouette and its details in gold, its brilliant ceramics, glittering mirrors and lattice windows. Behind the slim and lofty columns, painted in pale blue, stood the intricate glass stalactites and stalagmites crowning the golden gate leading to the tomb. Tiffaha had never seen anything so dazzling and felt a compelling urge to go down the couple of marble steps and risk entering the place. Yet the penalty could be very serious for a non-Muslim woman who set foot on this Muslim holy ground with no male companion. Not realizing who she was, a *sayid* with his imam headgear of red and green called to her, 'Come in, come in, my sister. I'll accompany you and lead you in prayer. Imam al-Kadhim will solve all your problems.'

Tiffaha thanked him but darted away like a frightened gazelle into the market in the direction of the southern gate of the mausoleum to have another look at the shrine from a different angle. The eastern side of the structure was lined with a series of lofty alcoves with pointed arches of typical Islamic design. The surface was covered with richly decorated ceramic tiles in brilliant shades of blue, yellow and red, but giving an overall impression of calm, misty blue. The raised alcoves afforded sitting space for scholars busy with their books, mostly the Holy Koran. At the back were the carved-oak doors to the inner living- and sleeping-rooms for the *sayids*, scholars and VIP visitors of the cloth. Tiffaha entered the shrine with grave misgivings, but she was so overwhelmed by the beauty of the place that she could not tear herself away.

The mosque's flocks of pigeons flew up from their perches as the clock struck the hour. Mrs Sassoon remembered Karim and rushed back to the taxi rank but his blue and yellow Chevrolet was nowhere to be seen. She had missed him, so total had been her preoccupation with the mosque, and she had to wait all over again. To and fro she walked, determined this time to keep the taxi rank within sight. Karim drew in after a few minutes and picked her up.

'Strange call! But where to, madam,' he asked in a tone of surprise and bewilderment.

'Take me somewhere out of town, somewhere among the palm groves where we won't be seen.'

A bold suggestion! Is she so frustrated as to come all this way from Karrada to Kadhimiah in the middle of the day for a bit of sex? He asked himself this question like any other frustrated Iraqi in a similar situation would have done. He smiled and drove away as suggested. The town of Kadhimiah is perched on the Karkh side of the Tigris River, with lovely sandy beaches fringed by thick palm-tree orchards all but deserted by the townspeople during the day. Throwing a thick cloud of exhaust fumes behind it over the winding earth embankment, the taxicab finally ended up in a well-secluded corner at the Fahhama Plantation. Only the odd fishing boat could be seen far away on the river every now and then. On the other side of the Tigris, some two hundred metres away, was the old water pump, drawing water to the orange and lemon groves beyond. The sound of the puffing chimney, 'Puff!

Puff! Puff!' gave a musical rhythm to this strange rendezvous between a man and a woman, a taxi driver and a middle-aged Jewish lady. Tiffaha, now far from the suspicious eyes of the Kadhimiah inhabitants, shed her *abaya* and tucked it down by her side.

'Now tell me, Karim, are you attached now? Married to someone nice?'

Oh, yes, here it comes, said the young driver to himself – just as I thought.

'No, madam. I am still a bachelor. I can't afford the dowry.'

'Well, Karim. I have a proposition for you. I can trust you, I know. But you must keep it very secret.'

Oh, yes. Here it is! 'Madam Tiffaha, I am no telltale. I won't mention a word of it to anyone.'

'We know you well. You are a very honest man. We can rely on you.'

Karim didn't like this plural pronoun, 'we'. It was time for her to drop it.

'You know the trouble with my husband?'

'Oh, yes. I am aware of it. Plenty of frustration for you, I am sure. A woman in the prime of her life having to cope with such a misfortune.'

'How right you are. You have no idea how frustrated I feel sometimes.'

'Oh, you don't need to tell me, Tiffaha. I can imagine what it feels like. I can see that – coming all the way from al-Sadun to Kadhimiah to find me.'

'To see him in this condition, getting worse from

day to day! I must take him out of this country. Jews
can no longer live here. Karim – help us by driving
us to the Iranian border. I'll make it worth your
while. We'll pay you any amount of money you want,
certainly enough for the most desirable woman's
dowry.'

The colour of Karim's complexion and the expression he wore changed dramatically. His lips
twisted and his eyes closed slightly like the eyes of a
pigeon dropping off to sleep. It was his turn to feel
frustration. The unexpected nature of her proposal
entailed a mixture of joy and sorrow, hope and disappointment, danger and adventure. The money was
tempting but the illegal operation was also dangerous.

'We are told that the best escape route for a Jew in
Baghdad is across the Shat al-Arab estuary from
Basra to the palm orchards around the port of
Muhammara in Iran. You only have to drop us in the
northern suburbs of Basra as close as possible to
the estuary embankment. We'll find our way across.
There are boatmen there who earn their living by
smuggling Jews at night. We'll bribe the police if we
meet them.'

'I know the area. I used to work there, smuggling
tobacco and tea. It is an area full of smugglers and
army deserters masquerading as poor fishermen. We
would go loaded with tea and tobacco and come back
piled high with hashish.'

Tiffaha was delighted with his willingness and,

indeed, enthusiasm for the project. In Iraq, a man can only get rich by defying the law and a Jew can only get anywhere by paying somebody. They agreed not to settle on any fee for the venture but to pay him at their discretion according to whatever trouble Karim would have to go to, plus any money he might have to pay to the border police for letting him drive on. The time for the departure was fixed for Saturday morning because the police did not expect the Jews to travel on the Sabbath. Karim drove Mrs Sassoon all the way back to Abdul Salam's surgery in Battaween, declining to take any fare for the journey. 'No. This is on the house.'

He helped Tiffaha carry the basket of pomegranates up the stairs to the surgery. Victoria was busy typing letters, which attracted the attention of the cab driver. He stared at the blonde Christian secretary and watched what she was doing with admiration. 'You write with a machine. Not with a pencil.'

'Yes. Typewriter,' she smiled.

'I also work with a machine. I drive a car,' he added amicably, coming gingerly a few more steps towards her. 'What do they call you?'

'My name is Victoria.'

'And I am Karim. My car is called Chevrolet.'

Victoria smiled in reply.

There was a pause of a few moments before the young man ventured to chip in with an enterprising suggestion. 'Could you teach me how to type? I can teach you how to drive in return.'

'That's an idea,' the young secretary giggled pleasantly and touched her golden hair.

✿ 11 ✿

To the Isle of Pigs

It was in Babylon and not in Palestine, Arabia or Egypt that the bulk of the Old Testament was drafted and the foundations of Judaism and monotheism were laid, a fact which explains the widespread belief that some three hundred biblical prophets are buried in Mesopotamia. As the Euphrates River is blessed with the shrine of the prophet Ezekiel, its twin river, the Tigris, on the other side of the valley, takes pride in having the sacred bones of yet another holy man, Ezra the scribe, buried on its eastern bank.

Under the single electric bulb lighting the entrance of the humble shrine, Karim drew in his cab to offer his two exhausted passengers a chance to visit the prophet and take some refreshment, readily supplied by barefoot street urchins bellowing with their harsh voices, 'Sherbet, sherbet! Laban, laban! Chay taza!' The Jewish couple waited for a few Arab peasants to leave the shrine in their dingy white *dishdashas* with haloes of the black *iqal* around their heads before they ventured in. The peasants looked surprised at the sight of the well-dressed urban couple and goggled at the lady with no *hijab* over her head or all-enveloping *abaya* to preserve her modesty. It was a long time since any Jew had made a call on Ezra. The bewilderment was reciprocal as the Sassoons had rarely seen such wretched, unshod and sick-looking creatures in the country. Were they really the same people who supplied the shops, hotels and posh restaurants with their eggs, milk, butter, vegetables and all that is delicious and desired?

The brick-built, low cubicle, no higher than two or three metres, looked in a very sorry state, desperately in need of a miracle, which Ezra had not so far managed to arrange. Despite the darkness of the night, especially chosen as a good cover for this nocturnal adventure, the river mysteriously shimmered behind the tomb, a charmless combination of mosque and synagogue. A few palm trees reached their long leaves in silhouette into the night sky, trying to draw down some of the bright stars clinging playfully to the firmament, oblivious to whatever was happening down below. The air was warm and heavy with the sour smell of dung and swampy water, which buffeted at the nose and throat. None of the senses was spared as the radio was blaring with songs and music from its corner in the *chaikhana*, the local café kept by Abu Khalil. The song was intermingled with the voice of a woman wailing somewhere at a distance, lamenting the loss of a dear soul or getting beaten up by another dear soul.

Ezra made the first clarion call of Zionism when he pressed the Babylonian Jews, some two thousand five hundred years ago, to return to the land of their ancestors in Israel and maintain their nationhood and sense of Jewishness. Dr Sassoon did not subscribe to the idea and was content to stand aside and let Tiffaha go in by herself and recite a few solemn words, waiting with a forced smile on his face, grim and vacant as it was. The chauffeur went right in and made a full circuit of the tomb without any notion as to the identity of the resident of the holy grave. It must have been, he rightfully thought, someone holy enough to justify building him a shrine. If Jews visited it then it must be someone with a certain amount of clout.

'This is one of your prophets, Doctor Sassoon,' he said to Abdul Salam as he went around his motor car to check the condition of its tyres and top up its radiator with fresh water from the café in this hot part of the country. With a piece of rag, he opened the radiator cap carefully and allowed the steam to shoot up safely in a thin jet without hurting himself. The vehicle was covered with dust which the thoughtful driver tried to wipe off with his hands. Some local street urchin had written in the dust on the boot 'Bloody Jews!' 'Get in, doctor, and let us go.'

The cab, however, had not moved more than a few metres on its way to Imara and Basra before one of the natives, hair dishevelled and eyes charged with agitation, threw himself in its path. 'For mercy's sake, doctor, have a look at my old mother and tell us what is wrong with her.' The young man in his *dishdasha* and worn-out sandals must have heard Karim addressing the doctor and thought at once of his ailing mother. There was no way for the driver to resume his journey, hard as he might have tried. The old, dusty street was soon turned into a make-shift hospital as the villagers brought their mothers and fathers, sterile women, disabled children and the dying to be examined and treated by Dr Sassoon. One old woman brought her famished cow. 'For Ezra's sake, can you prescribe something for her? She is hardly giving us any milk.' It took two hours at least before Dr Abdul Salam could sort out the medical problems of the area and Karim could re-start his engine and get on his way. On his lap rested a large piece of white cheese wrapped up in a cloth which the villagers had presented to the doctor in appreciation of his services.

The travellers crossed the iron bridge over the Kahla tributary to the sleeping city of Imara and passed by the Qal'at Salih townlet in the direction of al-Qurna where the Euphrates River joined its twin, the Tigris, and formed the mighty Shat al-Arab, over which so many nations had fought. It was almost dawn by the time the three travellers reached the outer suburbs of Basra, Iraq's only port and point of access to the Persian Gulf. It was a day in which visibility was reduced by a desert storm, a common phenomenon in this region of the Middle East. Karim had to find out from a street sweeper in which direction lay the Basra Royal Hospital where Dr George Malik, Abdul Salam's old friend from the Faculty of Medicine, was working. Dr Malik was stunned to see his erstwhile colleague turn up like that with a piece of white cheese in his hand, a much sadder and perplexed man, clearly in the throes of acute anxiety and inner suffering. But he could easily guess the purpose of the unexpected call so early in the morning. 'Yes,' he whispered to Tiffaha, 'I know a man who can lead you to a safe crossing place.' The Sassoons and their driver had to spend the day and night at George's comfortable house before attempting to cross the border to Iran over the Shat al-Arab estuary.

It was a sweet and bitter night for the two friends. 'The country has simply gone mad, but our people here will regret what they have done to the Jews. They are a terrible loss to Iraq.' George Malik shook his head as he spoke as if to expel some ghastly thoughts, like the undigested remnants of a mutton meal. Having heard all the unhappy episodes of the last few months while they dined, Dr Malik picked up his violin to soothe his guest when the meal was concluded; but no sooner had he played one or two notes than he was stopped by his friend. Abdul Salam Sassoon felt his chest aching with a sensation he had never experienced before. He put his hand, shaking and trembling, on the strings to silence the instrument and started to cry. Tears found their way down the furrows of both cheeks. 'Losing your country is worse than losing your beloved woman.' Dr Malik nodded in consent and started to feel his own tears welling up.

No one could sleep that night in George Malik's villa. This was convenient, for the travellers had an appointment with fate at the time of the early call for the Muslim dawn prayer. They hugged, they kissed and they wept their goodbyes. George Malik saw them to the end of the road in the small hours of the morning.

Against the vast watery expanse of Shat al-Arab, gleaming in the first shafts of early-morning light, Karim could make out the figures of two young men waving to them and urging them to come down to the water's edge. They had two short-oared metal boats tied up to an iron post. One of the two boatmen, the older and darker of the two, had all his front teeth set in gold, and they glittered like tiny Christmas lights as he smiled and welcomed his human cargo. 'Ahlan, ahlan.'

To him Taffaha addressed her anxious enquiry. 'You will take us across the water to the Iranian side?'

'Yes, sure.'

'In one of these things?' She expressed the doubt

which rose in her mind as she craned her neck to examine the tiny metal boats, probably handmade in haste specifically for these smuggling errands and each in appearance the size and shape of an open coffin. The younger boatman, lanky but broad shouldered, answered her with a sturdy kick by way of reassurance directed at the boat. The boat felt the impact of the kick and didn't like it at all. It bounced, turned and tried to get away, but the strong rope frustrated its intention. It just went on keeling from right to left and left to right until it settled down at last. Boats are meant for service and obedience not for revolt and revolution.

'It will cost you twenty-five dinars to take you to the other side, ten for us and fifteen for the police to close their eyes and let you go,' said the man with the gold teeth. 'And you will have to spend a night midway at the fishermen's cottage on the Isle of Pigs, before you get picked up by another boat to take you to the Iranian side. You will be met by a representative of the Jewish Agency. There will be other Jews to join you. The river has been very busy with the people of Moses in recent months.'

'Some people,' the second and younger boatman interjected, 'have changed the name of the island. They don't call it the Isle of Pigs any more. It is now the Jews' Island.'

While this exchange was going on in whispered tones, police or no police, Karim was busy loading and unloading the small quantity of the Sassoons' luggage, including Abdul Salam's pills, and securing everything in the tiny skip of a boat. Tiffaha handed over the twenty-five dinars to Abu Hamid, the older boatman, and paid Karim the money he was owed. He kissed both of them, bade them a final farewell and wished them good luck. They needed it. Tiffaha reciprocated and wished him well and a good homely wife, *bint halal*.

The travellers settled in the aft section, where Tiffaha snuggled into her sick husband's side gently and held his wrist. As Salman, the younger boat-man, gave a good push to the loaded boat and the ramshackle craft drifted away from the land of Iraq, both passengers looked back with tears swelling in their bewildered eyes. Abdul Salam felt his throat tightening and was unable to suppress a plaintive moan. There was only Karim on the shore to wave goodbye to them. The siren of the dockyard was heard ushering in the morning shift and the dockers and workers converged from every direction. The air was steaming hot and the sweat gathered in little droplets on the boatman's forehead and arms. The moisture trickled down under his shirt and pants as he attended to his business, baring his golden teeth and biting his lips.

The oars beat the calm water in their habitual rhythm, in and out. Every time they were raised from the water strings of glittering pearls fell from their flat ends back on to the rippling surface, pale ochre like the colour of their boatman, Abu Hamid, and the majority of the natives. He steered the fourteen-foot vessel with his oars up the river to bypass the strong current before venturing to cross and drifting back towards the jungle of the Isle of Pigs. Changing his position, Abu Hamid drew one oar into the boat and used the other as a pole to push his boat over the muddy shallows until it hit the bank with a gentle thud. 'Here we are all safe and sound.'

A semi-naked young man with a powerful, hairy chest and long black braids, wearing nothing other than grubby underwear and ex-army boots, emerged from the thicket and appeared before them like a Tarzan in Arab pants. Tiffaha grabbed her husband's arm and whispered some reassuring words in his ear. 'He is not a soldier. No, not a soldier.' Abdul Salam was on the verge of collapsing from the swirl of agonies churning in his belly as his wife led him out of the boat, which Abu Hamid was holding fast while standing in the murky water up to his knees. A colony of frogs took no notice of them and went on croaking among themselves as loudly as ever. They sat about with their big eyes, bold and shining, bulging out of their disproportionate heads.

'Yes, I know you. Two more Jews leaving Iraq. We counted three dozen kafirs, followers of your faith, yesterday,' shouted the Tarzan in pants as he helped the Sassoons to land and carry their scanty luggage.

He led the way through narrow paths between the tall grass, reeds and thorny shrubs and round stagnant puddles. Wild ducks in their flamboyant colours and other birds of different plumage flew away in panic, beating the air with their wings with a noisy clapping sound. Some turned towards the palm orchards of the town of Muhammara on the left bank. Others headed to the minarets of Basra. The path gradually gained width and finally opened up into a spacious clearing in the centre of the island. In the middle of the open space stood the humble shrine of a holy imam for whose blessings the fishermen, huntsmen and smugglers paid homage and gave offerings. It was a strange thing for a Muslim holy man to choose to live and die among the wild boars on a pigs' island and to get buried in soil mixed with pigs' shit. So thought this Jewish woman as she walked around the modest structure of baked bricks, its single window hung with green ribbons of supplication. 'Surely the man will rise on the Day of Judgement to face the Almighty Allah with all his bones soaked in pigs' urine and shit.'

In the midst of the Isle of Pigs, the small community of fishermen, huntsmen, army deserters and professional smugglers had built a hut of palm fronds over a structure of empty petrol cans filled with earth and pebbles, serving as bricks and stones. The modest hut was divided into two parallel sections, one for the Iranians and one for the Iraqis. As the

smugglers did not recognize any frontier demarc-
ation, they sat and slept wherever they liked. Arabs,
Iranians and Indians shared their food and conversed
in Arabic, Farsi, Hindi and some English. As it
stood, the improvised hut was, therefore, a genuine
embodiment of globalization, free enterprise and the
free market. The dealers bought and sold everything
from tea and coffee to marijuana and opium. From
time to time, one could even purchase pornographic
material and ladies' underwear. Anything went in this
little nest of global merchandise. Nothing was barred.
Even policemen and naval cadets used to come here
in their military boats and purchase whatever they
needed at special prices – to them,

'Salaam alykum,' Abdul Salam and Tiffaha saluted
the score of men inside the hut but received no reply to
their salutation for the fishermen and smugglers were
at prayer.

However, the imam, a regular smuggler, raised his
voice in recognition, 'Al-hamdu lillahy rab al-alamin.'
Praise be to Allah, the god of mankind.

With their worship rituals solemnly performed,
the men made room for the couple of strangers and
invited them to share a morsel of food with them.

'By Allah, it is all halal, fish straight from the
river.'

The Sassoons were grateful and offered to pay for
their meal, but the fishermen would not have it. It
was all on the house.

'In Iran, we have no problem with the Jews,' said one of the fishermen in broken Arabic and even more broken English. 'They are always welcome.'

'My uncle, Abdul Hussein . . . '

The speaker could not complete his sentence for another fisherman interrupted him. 'To be sure our Shah, so I heard from a friend, is a Jew. His grandmother was a Jewess.'

The man was immediately cut short by a more knowledgeable colleague. 'No, no. It was not his grandmother but the aunt of his grandmother. And that is why he likes the Jews and cooperates with Israel.'

The conversation went on and on, to and fro, with the final conclusion being that all the kings and heads of state in the Middle East shared a Jewish origin.

Finding the subject tedious and unrewarding, Ahmad Ali, an Iranian fisherman with a bald head like the skin of a watermelon and a loud voice to match, burst out singing and put an end to all that disputation about the origins of the Middle Eastern rulers. He sang loud and clear one *dasht* after another and finished with a popular *pasta* in a very upbeat rhythm. His mates clapped and joined in or simply sang solo in Arabic or Farsi. Only the Indians kept their peace and just pretended to be listening. With the singing session concluded they all got up and went their separate ways. Only Abdul Salam, Tiffaha and the Arab Tarzan were left, and the three took their places on the straw mats covering the floor and slept, but only for a few minutes.

'I did not kill her! I swear I didn't! No, no, I didn't kill her.' Abdul Salam shouted his protestations with a rasping gusto and interrupted their sleep, while kicking with his legs and throwing his hands in the air, like an infant with midnight colic. 'No, no, no! I swear I did not kill her.'

'Shush! Shush! It's all right. It's all right.'

Abdul Salam woke up from his nightmare with his face convulsed with terror and breathing spasmodically. He looked towards his wife pitifully, grabbed her arm and buried his plaintive face between her slender neck and shoulder. She could hear his agitated heart beating against her own, which prompted her to put her hand gently on his chest.

An hour later and the drama was resumed all over again. Mrs Sassoon had become quite accustomed to the ordeal. 'Take no notice of him,' she reassured the Arab Tarzan. 'He's only dreaming.'

'He repeats the same dream – killing somebody, perhaps some woman?' queried Tarzan-in-pants in a suspicious tone.

'Yes, he is a gynaecologist. So many women die under the scalpel of surgeons. Take no notice of what he says. He is only having a bad dream.'

But Tarzan-in-pants couldn't sleep and was the first to rise. With the early light of day he started to ferry the baggage to the new boat on the other side of the Isle of Pigs, ready to cross over to the Iranian shore. The left side of the river was a narrow and shallow strip of calm water which Tarzan could ford with his bare feet, pulling the boat behind him. With that operation done, Dr Abdul Salam Sassoon stepped out on the Iranian soil and looked behind him. 'Thank God,' Tiffaha whispered to herself as the couple saw the last of the country of their birth, scene of their falling in love, their marriage and their final tribulations, a land which they would never see again. They turned to Tarzan and tipped him for his pains before climbing up the embankment into the palm orchard where they were met by a representative of the Jewish Agency.

'Welcome to Iran, gateway to Israel.'

The Sassoons' onward journey to Eretz Israel was destined to lead north-east from Muhammara and Abadan, the great oil centre of Iran, to Dezful, the religious centre of Qum and finally to Teheran, along the bare Karkha valley and over the rugged mountains of western Iran, avoiding the Pusht-e-Kuh range to the west. Abdul Salam slept soundly on the back seat of the swaying cab throughout the long and tiring night journey. He did not even wake up at the numerous stops on the way to relieve himself like the rest of his fellow travellers. But they were kind enough to fetch fresh *istikans* of strong tea for the woman companion whenever the cab stopped by a roadside café.

The great synagogue of Abarishmi in Teheran was kept busy with the immigrants from Iraq. Rabbi Moshe found ample time to listen to the doctor and his wife and their tale of woe. 'Don't think that I am a superstitious old man,' the ancient cleric with his henna-dyed beard said to Tiffaha, speaking first in Hebrew; but, noticing that they didn't understand, he went on to finish his advice in broken Arabic of the Baghdadi Jewish dialect, garnished with Farsi words. 'What I advise you to do is to take your husband to Isfahan, spend a night in the Chopara district of the Jews and seek the blessings of Ezekiel. He will rid your husband of his affliction. Iran is full of people, Jews and Muslims and, mind you, Christians also, who would have given up but for the sacred power of the blessed Prophet Ezekiel.'

'But we have taken him to his shrine.'

'Where? In Isfahan?'

'No, no, in his proper grave in al-Kifil, in Iraq.'

The rabbi screwed up his eyes and beat the air with both hands in a gesture of utter despair. He scratched his face and pulled at his ginger beard before being capable of a coherent reply. 'This is false! This is an Arab lie. The Arabs are notorious liars. They claim they have in Iraq the graves of all our prophets and blessed scribes. Utter nonsense!' Rabbi Moshe tugged his beard again in support of his vehement assertion, delivered with a genial sarcastic smile, 'Utter nonsense. They are all buried here in Iran, the land of

King Cyrus. This is where Daniel and Aster are buried. There is only one Ezekial and he is buried here in Isfahan.' Listening to the reverent rabbi, the Sassoons began to believe that the whole of Judaism was born and developed in Persia. The whole story of the Exodus from Egypt was no more than a Babylonian concoction. The true exodus was from Iran.

Abdul Salam, who had some saliva gathering around his trembling lips, felt his chest tightening. Tiffaha was less perturbed and smiled with the thought that probably there was a third Ezekiel buried somewhere in Boston or Manhattan – an American Ezekiel; and perhaps there was a British Ezekiel and a Franco-German Ezekiel. Ezekiels of all shapes and colours. Who knows?

Yet Rabbi Moshe won the argument and the couple delayed their departure to Israel and spent two days with the Persian Ezekiel of Isfahan in a Muslim mosque richly decorated with ceramic tiles in the Iranian style. Having performed that ritualistic task, the Sassoons returned to Teheran and took a taxi forthwith to the Teheran International Airport. The two-engined aeroplane roared and lifted them up finally from the land of Islam, together with a crowd of fellow Iraqi Jews travelling on the same magic carpet, first of all westwards in the direction of Cyprus and then back again to the shores of the promised land.

❧ 12 ☙

By the Shores of the Sea of Galilee

Contradictions. Israel seemed to be a land full of contradictions. A land of peace drenched in blood. In this sunny part of the world, the sky was dark and the rain fell incessantly and turned the thirsty ground into a quagmire. Not a very auspicious beginning for the new arrivals from all four corners of the world. Mud was engulfing the hundreds of tents and temporary premises allocated to the immigrants from Iraq and Iran. The heavy rain, however, did not stop the Iraqis from braving the weather or the Jewish Agency by demonstrating against both the Almighty and the authorities. The improvised placards were dripping on the protesters as they chanting: 'Down with Zionism.'

'Long live the world revolution.'

'Send us back.'

'We want houses, not empty promises.'

Rain or no rain, some of the Iraqi immigrants found a great deal of pleasure in marching in demonstrations and shouting defiant slogans without being arrested or shot at. The limited skirmishes with the Israeli police did not go beyond a slanging match involving 'Bloody Zionists' and 'Bloody Communists'. Some of the immigrants were thinking of going back without knowing how, while the Jewish Agency officers were doing their best to calm them down by promising them better days to come.

The 'Magic Carpet Operation' which transferred the Iraqi Jews to Israel was not just a historical operation but also a hysterical undertaking. Iraqi legislation, which allowed the Jews to cancel their Iraqi nationality and go to Israel, gave the hundred-and-thirty-thousand-strong Jewish community one year only in which to register and leave the country. In 1951, the Jewish state itself was merely three years old, with all the problems associated with the birth of a new nation. There were no homes ready for all the immigrants with their children and old people. Everything had to be improvised, primarily housing. Thousands of tents and wooden shacks had to be set up for the newcomers as they came from the airliners with nothing other than the most essential baggage. The Iraqi Jews were highly educated and well qualified. They made up one of the most picturesque, capable and sophisticated Jewish communities in the world, something which the Western Ashkenazi establishment took years to recognize. There was a hint of racism against the Orientals in disregarding their degrees and diplomas and ignoring their talents and qualifications. Only menial jobs were allocated to

them, arousing their anger and their instant resent-
ment. One orange picker protested that he was
treated worse than his donkey, whose shift ended at
four o'clock while he had to go on working until five.
The German reparations of millions of dollars were
not available yet and the United States allowed
the Jewish state at that time only meagre assistance
with the economy as weak as it was. The threat of
annihilation by the Arabs was also more serious and
immediate then. Everything had to be prioritized and
housing was not a priority politically.

Abdul Salam Sassoon was puzzled by the demonstrations and for some time he thought that he was
still in Iraq, especially when he heard some of the
shouting in Arabic, or more precisely Jewish Arabic.
The newcomers did not know much Hebrew beyond
the few words with religious connotations. The
slogans, therefore, were written in improvised
Hebrew, English, Arabic, Farsi and even Kurdish. It
was only when he noticed that the police did not open
fire or attack the demonstrators, that Abdul Salam
realized that he was no longer in Iraq. The sight of
the demonstrations, however, prompted him to leave
his wife behind and join in. It was a hard task for
Tiffaha to drag him out and take him to a café near
by where they could watch without getting involved.
Rumours spread that the Iraqi Communists were
acting on instructions from the Kremlin to wreck
the progress of the young Jewish state. The Soviet

leaders, who at the outset were apparently persuaded that the Jewish state would follow the course of socialism and communism, were disappointed with the outcome. Stalin took revenge by liquidating his Jewish advisers and inspired the Israeli Communist Jews to make life difficult for the Israeli establishment, clearly a bunch of stooges of American imperialism. Abdul Salam was on the verge of getting sucked into this affair when his wife received a letter from the Israeli public health authorities.

The Ashkenazi Jews coming from Europe and America took it for granted that the other Jews coming from countries of the Third World would be almost as fit and healthy as they were. But they were soon disabused by the heavy medical demands of the Arab Jews, Indian Jews, Iranian Jews and even black African Jews with frizzy hair and dark skin. They apparently expected Zionism to deal with all their woes, treat their stomach ulcers, hiatus hernias, tuberculosis, infertility and even sexual impotence. Eretz Israel, they thought, would have a cure for everything, but Abdul Salam Sassoon had to wait for five months before he could see anyone. Madness was not an urgent case in Israel. 'Everyone is mad here.' The country was also flooded, it must be remembered, with the hordes of traumatized people who were the surviving victims of Nazi Germany.

Yet the consultant thought that Sassoon's case called for some special and urgent treatment. The referred man, after all, was not an ordinary madman but a mad gynaecologist. He was, therefore, admitted speedily to the mental department of the Hadassah Hospital. They didn't have a special section for mad gynaecologists so they put him in the general ward, between a new immigrant from the United States who had developed the conviction that he was an ass soon after his arrival and a paranoid old man who suffered severe anxiety that someone was going to get him married to an Arabian mare. Every time the young American started braying as all asses, genuine or fake, frequently do, the old man cried with his eyes popping out of their sockets, 'No, no . . . please, I don't want her!' Abdul Salam, out of his own despair, would then shout abusive Arabic at both of them, and the two would think that this fellow between them spoke the language of the devil. The slanging trio would then turn the whole clinic into a real bedlam. Abdul Salam Sassoon complained to his wife, 'You know this place is going to make me mad,' which was not very far from the truth. But he had to endure the place for nearly three months. Instead of getting any better he was manifestly getting worse.

She was feeling guilty, wondering whether it had been sensible of her to seek a remedy for an insane Jew by uprooting him and bringing him to Israel. Was it right, she asked herself repeatedly, to have cut off her husband from his roots in Iraq, the country where he was born, had experienced love and received his education, in order to bring him to an alien environment which had no resonance for him other than religious mythology? In the circumstances, she decided to apply to the hospital to have him released into the care of his spouse. The psychiatrist in charge was more than willing to sign his discharge papers. Tiffaha collected his things, including Karl Marx's *Das Capital*, and took him out.

'Thank you, my dear,' he murmured to his wife with a loving smile on his face. 'This was really useful. The three months I have spent here have given me the only opportunity in my life to understand Uncle Marx's *Das Capital*.'

Medics always stick together. Thus the Hadassah Hospital went out of its way to request the housing department to house the Sassoons in accommodation suitable for his condition and his position as a medical consultant. A large empty house was found for them in the town of Tiberias on the Sea of Galilee. The house was a mixture of the West and the Orient. The ground floor consisted of two reception rooms, a large kitchen and a bathroom with its own heating system, based on paraffin oil. The first floor had two bedrooms with a balcony overlooking the Sea of Galilee. When the representative of the Jewish Agency showed them round the place, which stood on a pleasant slope of the hills, they found all the rooms well furnished and decorated with many pictures on the walls, including one showing the Dome of the

Rock. There were also some framed examples of Arabic calligraphy on the walls of one reception room.

'Yes. Ayat al-Kursi from the Koran,' Abdul Salam whispered to his wife.

'I see you can read Arabic. I can't. They say it is very similar to Hebrew. But I really can't see any similarity except that they both run from right to left. Anyway we shall have these pictures removed.'

'To whom did this place belong?'

'It belongs to us now, but I have no idea who lived here last.'

With a vague grin on his face the Jewish Agency representative sidled up to Tiffaha to whisper something which he obviously deemed confidential. 'Mrs Sassoon, it will help your husband if you can manage to persuade him to change his name. I mean his two personal names, Abdul Salam. This is what I was told in the hospital. The consultant told me that it would undoubtedly help him to recover his sanity if he dropped his Arabic name.'

'He said that?' Tiffaha whispered back, pressing her hand to her heart.

'You know, people here might think that he is a Communist, coming from Iraq with a name like that. A Hebrew name would sound more appropriate, more loyal to the Jewish state.'

'Yes, we did think of that but he was dead against it.'

'What a shame.'

To skip away from the subject, Mrs Sassoon bent down to examine the Persian carpet on the floor of the sitting-room. The rest of the floors, including that of the kitchen, were covered with colourful tiles with geometric patterns in black, white, brown and flamboyant green. The Sassoons were exceedingly lucky to be housed in a place which was already so well furnished and equipped. It saved them a lot of time, money and effort. They only had to fetch their suitcases and move in straight away. The balcony was a veritable boon for Abdul Salam, who adopted the habit of spending every morning sitting there, chin resting on the wooden parapet, watching the sun rising from the east over the Golan Heights and listening to the birds perched in the eucalyptus trees singing their hearts out. The Sea of Galilee was always busy with boats of all kinds, which Abdul Salam liked to watch. Nothing more peaceful, you would think.

'You know what I really miss here?' he said as he was taking a cup of coffee from his wife.

'What is that, darling?'

'The sight of storks on minarets.'

❦ 13 ❧

A Stranger at the Door

The air was mild and the Sea of Galilee was ablaze with the fiery rays of the setting sun, so that the water seemed to be rippling with gold from the first-floor windows where Abdul Salam was standing and observing the majestic scene before him. The Golan Heights on the other side of this Lake of Tiberias were dressed up for the occasion in a pale purple garment. Straight and motionless, the cypress, eucalyptus and poplar trees seemed themselves thrilled with this bold review of colours: violet, purple, scarlet and restful pale ultramarine. Abdul Salam seemed more cheerful and his demeanour less agitated as he put on his grey jumper to get ready for his evening walk with his wife. The calm was interrupted by a gentle and unexpected knocking at the front door. He heard his wife's voice exchanging some words with a stranger in Arabic, something which he had not heard often since his departure from Iraq.

'Who is it, my dear?'

'Someone who wants to talk to you.'

'To me?'

'Yes, darling. A Palestinian.'

Abdul Salam froze for a few moments before steeling himself to go downstairs to see the man. It was someone dressed differently and rather neatly. Dark ginger hair crowned a suntanned face with grey eyes and a hooked Semitic nose, which almost divided his thick moustache into two separate entities. He looked quite self-assured, despite the inward hesitation which he was trying to overcome.

'I am sorry, doctor, to trouble you,' he started politely in English with an American accent. 'I live in the States, an American citizen, but I was born in this house. I spent my childhood here before the exodus, that is the Palestinian exodus of 1948. I am sorry to mention that to you. But I am on a visit to my, I mean to your country to see some of those who remained behind – my uncle and cousins in Acre. It just dawned on me that I would like to see the place where I was born – just nostalgia, you know.'

'I understand.'

'Is it possible to have a look at the place, my old playroom? You know how memories sometimes draw you so that you can't resist.'

'I understand. Please come in, if you would like to. Come in and have a good look at the place. I really didn't know who owned the house or who lived here before. The authorities gave it to us. I am not well and they gave me this house to help me. You know what I mean.' Feeling at ease with the stranger,

Abdul Salam broke into Arabic with his Baghdadi dialect. 'I come originally from Iraq. You may find my Arabic language strange and hard to understand. But please come in.'

The face of this uninvited visitor radiated with delight. He had not expected anyone in the house to give him such an open and warm welcome.

'Darling, we have a visitor,' Abdul Salam called to Tiffaha. 'Can you make him a coffee while he goes around the house. It is an interesting story. He was born here and would like to refresh his memories.'

'Ahlan wa sahlan,' she said as she darted towards the kitchen to prepare the coffee.

The stranger went around the various rooms, upstairs and downstairs, but oddly enough he always returned to a certain corner in the kitchen. He would stand there for a while, obviously in agitation and sorrow, like a man standing on the edge of the grave of his beloved. His face would look vacant for a second and then tears would well in his eyes; his hands would tremble and the muscles in his jaw would seem to flutter. He looked as if he was soliciting some relief from these two people he hardly knew. Even the uninvolved doctor could sense there was something tormenting the visitor's mind. He had no option but to repeat himself kindly. 'I am sorry. I know you must feel very upset as you remember how you used to live and play in this place. Your childhood and . . . '

'I heard you are a doctor from Iraq and you seem

to be a very kind person. May I entrust you with this little anecdote – call it a report if you like.'

'Please don't worry. We know you must have a lot of things on your mind. Don't worry. I am also an Arab like you.'

'Dr Sassoon, I am standing now on a tile covering the whole history and wealth of my family.'

'Oh! I have noticed how you come back repeatedly to this spot here and stand on this tile.'

'Dr Sassoon, when our people ran away in 1948, they never thought that their flight would be so final. They thought it would be only a matter of a few weeks before the Arab armies came and reconquered the place and restored everything to us. On that fateful day my father gathered all the gold of the family, my mother's anklets and bracelets, his golden Longine watch, my sisters' necklaces and bracelets and all the valuable things in the house, including the gold sovereigns my father had saved. He lifted a tile, this tile I am standing on, and dug a hole and buried everything underneath it in safe keeping for their return.'

'This is the tile you are standing on now?'

'That's right.'

The Palestinian caller put his hand in his pocket and produced a tattered piece of paper which he showed to Dr Sassoon.

'My father drew a map of the layout of the house, indicating the position of that tile with the gold buried underneath. He kept the map with him, waiting for the Arab armies to come and liberate the land and restore mother's gold to her. Of course, this never happened. My father died but before his death he handed over the map to my Uncle Ahmad. When my uncle died soon after, it passed to his brother, Uncle Mustapha. The map changed hands, passing from one member of the family to another, all of them waiting and expecting the liberation of Palestine to restore my mother's gold to her, until it finally fell into my hands. Here it is. This is it.'

'All underneath your shoes.'

'That's right, underneath here.' The Palestinian exile stamped on the tile.

'And you came to recover the gold?'

'No. The gold belongs to the house and the house belongs to you now. My mother is a very old woman and she is sick with cancer. She may die any day now. But before she dies I want to give her this little pleasure, to bring her the golden anklets and tell her that the Arab armies have liberated Tiberias and we have got our gold back. You can have the rest of the gold, Dr Sassoon.'

Both Dr and Mrs Sassoon were almost in tears. Tiffaha could feel her heart thumping as her chest tightened with anguish. She looked at her husband and her husband looked at the man.

'No, my friend. We are not robbers to take somebody else's gold.'

As action seemed to be called for, he went to the garden forthwith and came back with a spade and an axe. He removed the tile and dug out the old hole carefully, like an archaeologist at a precious historical site, picking up the pieces one by one without damaging any of them. Tiffaha put them under the tap, washed them, dried them and neatly laid them on the table piece by piece. Abdul Salam put the Longine watch to his ear to see whether it was still ticking after all those years. The Sassoons and the visitor were in a dilemma as to the fate of the rest of the gold, but the couple were adamant they would not accept any part of the treasure.

'But you haven't drunk your coffee. Sit down and have your coffee while my wife wraps everything up for you and puts it in a bag. You can't walk around in Israel carrying precious gold in your hands. Sit down and tell us more about it. I mean, what exactly happened to your people in 1948. We were only briefed with what they wanted us to hear.'

Abdul Ghafur, for that was the name of the visitor, did not leave the house until the clock in the sitting-room struck the midnight hour. In the morning of the following day, it was Abdul Ghafur's turn to hear a knocking at the door of his room and it was Abdul Salam Sassoon who was the visitor this time. His insomnia had been worse than ever as he lay by his wife's side, thinking, remembering and sweating.

171

Every few minutes he felt his lungs bursting and his eyes working, opening and closing spasmodically beyond his control. Words gushed out of his trembling mouth but not with the blurred incoherence of dreams or nightmares. In that state of agitation, he lifted his head from the pillow and sat up until dawn.

'I am sorry, Abdul Ghafur, to call on you so early at the hotel. I just could not sleep after what you had told me. The massacre of Deir Yassin and how your sister perished. I just couldn't sleep,' Abdul Salam's words hung in the air, begging for a response. He swallowed and felt something burning in his throat.

The two men, strangers to each other, seemed locked together by an invisible chain. It was something akin to the thraldom of an old affair raising its head again and calling for a settlement. They left the hotel and spent the day walking, unaware of the direction they took or the passage of time. The following day they found themselves together again in Jerusalem, Jaffa, Haifa and Tel Aviv. These wanderings brought Abdul Salam into contact with Arabs, Palestinian Muslims and Christians as well as Israelis who wanted a different kind of Israel, a democratic state for both Jews and Arabs. Within the short spell of time they spent together, Abdul Salam Sassoon and Abdul Ghafur met bi-nationalists, Zionists and anti-Zionists, Communists, Trotskyites and peace lovers of all shades and kinds. After months of abstraction and befuddlement, Abdul Salam began to focus on something, and it was the injustice meted out to the natives of this land.

Abdul Ghafur went back to America but found himself in constant contact with his new Jewish friend, sometimes by the exchange of letters and other times over the telephone. The contact introduced Abdul Salam to various groups and individuals on both sides of the divide. He found himself sucked in gradually by politics which was by no means a new experience for him. He began to write articles in Arabic for *al-Ittihad* and other leftist Arabic publications and even joined a number of demonstrations for human rights. Abdul Ghafur's reference to his sister, who was massacred by the Zionist fanatics of the Stern terrorist gang together with nearly three hundred Palestinians – old men, women and children – who were dumped in an old well, inspired Dr Sassoon to pursue further enquiries into what exactly had happened in 1948. It did not take him long to ascertain that the Deir Yassin atrocity was accompanied by similar acts in Nasr al-Din, Saris, Yajur and other locations, perpetrated with the object of terrifying the Palestinians and forcing them to leave their homes and seek refuge in the neighbouring Arab countries. All in all, nearly three quarters of a million Palestinians had left their homes to begin the life of refugees maintained by the charity of the world community. The United Nations resolution to allow them back to their homes was swept aside and remained a mere scrap of paper. No attempt was made to persuade Israel to withdraw from the land it had captured in 1948 by force of arms, land beyond the territory earmarked for the Jews in the United Nations partition plan. Dr Sassoon was puzzled as to how such naked acts and obvious facts could be swept under the carpet by the Israeli media and the moulders of Jewish public opinion. Maybe the Israeli public did not want to know. They did not want to spoil the exultation, as it were, now that their dream of having their own Jewish state once more, an independent and triumphant state to which all Jews could go in time of need and trouble, had become a reality.

Mrs Sassoon regretted his decision to leave the comfortable house overlooking the Sea of Galilee allocated to him by the Israeli authorities and choose to live in one of the rough wooden shacks set up for the Jewish immigrants coming from Iraq and other Middle Eastern countries. But Tiffaha did not stand in his way because she found this new interest produced a welcome change for the better in her husband's mental state. Slowly but steadily he was regaining his former normality. He began to eat well, sleep well and feel more relaxed. To all intents and purposes, Dr Abdul Salam Sassoon was no longer unduly troubled in his mind, let alone mad. It is one of the peculiarities of the human race that great discoveries, achievements and turns for the better are often born out of the unhappiness and suffering of man. For one thing, Abdul Salam stopped repeating 'I did not kill her' to all and sundry. Such was his state of mind now that he was able to apply to be re-registered as a medical practitioner.

In her own mind Tiffaha Sassoon could not help asking herself how it was possible that after all his visits to the learned rabbis and sheikhs, and to the bones of Ezekiel, Ezra and several other prophets of the Old Testament, and likewise after all the medical prescriptions of drugs and ECT courses recommended by the best neurologists and psychiatrists in Baghdad and Jerusalem, her husband could achieve no appreciable improvement in his condition until he met this Palestinian stranger from New York? Could it be that through the power of the awakened conscience and commitment to the dictates of this power a human being may recover his wits, turn over a new leaf and lead a better life? Tiffaha brooded over this question time and time again in her mind, but like the good wife that she was she embraced her husband's new direction and felt immensely relieved to see him regaining his composure and looking forward to resuming his medical career.

❦ 14 ❧

Friends and Enemies

Abdul Salam Sassoon was a qualified gynaecologist with a distinguished British medical degree but somehow the Health Authorities in Tel Aviv didn't feel it was quite right to entrust Jewish wombs to the hands of a doctor with a mental record and medical experiences and qualifications from Baghdad. A more acceptable solution was found. He was commissioned as an army doctor charged with the task of looking after the Arab prisoners of war. Any mistake he might make would not shake the foundations of the state of Israel or reflect negatively on its medical standards.

Sassoon welcomed their decision as it brought him into direct contact with his former Arab roots to have patients who were Egyptian soldiers, Iraqis, Syrians and Jordanians. His senior officers did not approve of his close fraternization with the enemy, the Arab soldiers, but they overlooked this inclination and allowed for it on the grounds that he was half mad anyway. What sensible man in the world would enjoy the company of Arab army officers? With these Arab soldiers, he found ample time to play dominoes and backgammon. They turned the games into war games, in which he represented the Zionist enemy and they represented the armies of the Arab countries. It was a welcome change of mood for the prisoners to score some easy victories against the Israelis on the rickety coffee tables. After all, victory in the world of the Middle East is victory even if it is in plastic, wood or paper. It was such fun that even the other senior officers could not resist joining in or watching the progress, calling, shouting and encouraging. It was almost the real thing. Every time Abdul Salam lost, the officers would go home feeling depressed and deflated whereas the prisoners of war would enjoy the rare taste of victory. It was good for the Arabs to find themselves beating the Israelis in something, albeit dominoes or backgammon. Another diversion was musical. Dr Sassoon managed to purchase an oud, the father of all Arabic music and all string instruments, and pass most of his leisure time reviving his musicality and playing or singing with the prisoners, especially those who came from Iraq. They actually formed a small band singing the classical Baghdadi *maqam* and the Iraqi pop songs of Salima Murad, Afifa Iskander, Aziz Ali and the rural melodies of Niles and Ubudias.

There was, however, the dietary problem of halal meat for the prisoners. Muslims may only eat meat that has been killed in the name of Allah. It is true that Muslims, Jews and Christians worship the same God, but they differ on meat. For all Muslims, it can only be halal when the animal is slain with the words, 'Bism Allah al-rihman al-rahim.' A meeting of the older prisoners recommended that an imam be appointed to ensure the halal quality of the food. An Egyptian sergeant-major volunteered to act as an imam. But a Shi'i soldier from Iraq took exception to a Sunni sheikh who did not conclude with a mention of Imam Ali, Wali Allah. Misbah al-Din, a prisoner of war from Jordan, proposed to bring Sheikh Shams al-Din from Amman every morning to bless the sheep or chickens and turn their flesh into good halal meat. Murad abu Khubuz, a young lieutenant from southern Egypt, suggested bringing a sheikh from al-Azhar University of Cairo to supervise the slaying operation and make sure that the carcases were properly bled according to the sharia before cooking the meat with all the offal. While the Israeli contractors continued to supply kosher provisions, the Arabs went on arguing about it among themselves.

The matter was finally settled when a Sephardi rabbi from Jerusalem brought a thick volume of sharia edicts. He turned to the page and pointed to the old fatwa, 'Eat with the Jews and sleep with the Christians.' Whereupon all the prisoners nodded their heads in consent and approval as they read what a man who lived centuries ago in some desert town had thought and written about the quality of meat and the rules of conduct. The Israeli contractors went on supplying the camp with their kosher meat.

'Excuse me, doctor, are you the same gynaecologist who had a practice in al-Sadun in Baghdad?' one of the Iraqi soldiers asked him. He was young, handsome and broad shouldered, tall and slim with hazel eyes and lush brown curls, the colour of a wet oak barrel, covering almost his entire forehead. His complexion was as pale as a white chocolate bar. The young man took a deep breath before he put his question. His eyes were wide open, anxious and hungry for a response. He spoke swiftly and jerkily. Once the words had escaped from his mouth it remained wide open as if he had lost all control of his lips. The other inmates were agog. For a fleeting second, Abdul Salam thought that this young fellow's face was not altogether unfamiliar to him. His eyes squinted and flicked up and down, scrutinizing the soldier in front of him. The awkward silence could not be maintained indefinitely. All those who sat around the rickety coffee table were waiting for a response to the question. The doctor felt that he was under a moral obligation to provide the young man with an answer.

'As a matter of fact,' he stammered, 'I happen to be of Iraqi origin. Yes, you are right. I had a medical practice in the al-Sadun district of Baghdad.'

Dr Sassoon thought that his answer would be the end of the subject but he was completely mistaken for the young Iraqi soldier put an even more demanding question. 'I thought so. Do you remember, in

Baghdad, doctor, a family by the name of Abd al-Ali?'

No sooner did the young man finish with his question than the doctor clutched his head as if to prevent it from falling on the concrete floor.

'You are . . . let me think . . . '

'Hassun Abd al-Ali,' blurted out the young prisoner of war as if to relieve the doctor and refresh his memory.

'My God! Fancy that! You missed an appointment with me in Baghdad, months or years ago, and now you come here to keep it. Fancy that! Who would ever have thought it?'

'I am glad, Dr Sassoon, that you are well now and back in the medical profession. But how is it that you are looking after us? You are a gynaecological consultant. We have no pregnant soldiers for you here. We have no women soldiers in the Arab armies as you have here in Israel.'

'I am a military doctor. Orders are orders in the armed forces. They said, you are in charge of the Arab prisoners of war, and so here I am, a doctor for the Arab prisoners of war.'

Abdul Salam Sassoon threw down the dice and gave up the game. 'I surrender. I have lost. I have something more important now. Come with me, Ha . . . sss . . . '

'Hassun. My name is Hassun. You have forgotten it. No matter.'

'Well, whatever it is come along with me, Hassun,

and tell me your story. Who put you in uniform and what brought you here to Israel, a prisoner of war in our hands, a prisoner in the hands of the Israeli army? Fancy that! Come to my surgery and let me hear your full story from A to Z.'

Dr Abdul Salam Sassoon took Private Hassun Abd al-Ali and led him to his humble surgery, produced two bottles of beer from the fridge, put Hassun on the couch and spent the rest of the day talking with him, exchanging notes and following up old stories from Baghdad, Basra, Isfahan, Teheran and finally the state of Israel. Abdul Salam described to him how he had crossed the Shat al-Arab estuary and spent a night on the Isle of Pigs with smugglers and army deserters. How a fisherman there asked him for a prescription to enlarge his penis. 'Sex! Sex! Sex! That is the only thing that matters to the people in this region. Rich or poor, young or old, they all gaze at their organ and measure its length.' Both men laughed. 'They worry about satisfying their women but they never really try to satisfy them.'

The course of the conversation drifted to the Arab–Israeli War and how Hassun was taken prisoner because of a failure of communication and lack of initiative. His platoon was surrounded by the Israeli forces but no one came to the rescue. The commanding officer was waiting for orders from his superior and his superior was waiting for instructions from Baghdad. The famous 'Maku

awamir'. No orders. 'They don't wait for orders
though when they want to bugger a little boy. They
show plenty of initiative then.'

The evening resulted in a daily pattern. As soon as
Dr Sassoon had finished his surgery work he was
joined by Hassun Abd al-Ali for the evening chat
under the ceiling fan which went on swishing and
paddling round and round as the temperature hit the
forties. The shrill cicadas on the inside seemed to be
listening to and competing with the crickets chirping
outside and the whining of the mosquitoes as they
went about the business of tormenting the inhabitants. A bottle of beer would be opened. A meze of
green olives and a bowl of salted peanuts would be
shared between them. They were generally by themselves but sometimes other prisoners of war from Iraq
joined in. With Abdul Salam bringing in his oud, the
army surgery was turned into a little music hall. The
doctor would play on the oud and others would do
the singing. They went through the whole classical
repertoire of Iraqi songs, especially the Jewish
melodies of Iraq's prima donna, Salima Murad:

> *Ya, nab'at al rihan,*
> *Hinni ala al-walhn.*
> *Jismi nihal,*
> *Wa al-ruh thabat,*
> *Wa adhmi ban.*

Oh, you plant of myrtle,
Show pity to the lover.
My body is weak,
My soul has withered,
My bones are sticking out.

When tired of music and singing, the two would talk nostalgically about the good old days of life in Baghdad. The life on the sandy beaches along the Tigres River at al-Karrada, the lively evenings in the cafés and bars dotting Abu Nuas Street, the *masquf* fish banquets, the rowdy entertainments provided by the old cabarets and the violent student demonstrations in Rashid Street and Bab al-Mu'addam Square. They discussed the momentous events which had shaped the contemporary history of Iraq and the Arab world. How General Bakr Sidqi, the Chief of Staff of the Iraqi Armed Forces, staged the first military coup in the Middle East and set up the example to be followed by the soldiers of other Arab countries. How Rashid Ali al-Gaylani declared war against Britain in May 1941 and how the Jews were subjected to the pogrom of Farhud in which so many of them were slain, raped and stripped of their belongings. Abdul Salam related to his listeners how Salma the belly-dancer was invited to entertain the army generals and was gang-raped by the officers. Of course, they moved on to discuss the unavoidable topics of Palestine, imperialism and Zionism. It was the intrusion of the Zionist Movement which wrecked the comfortable life of Middle Eastern Jewry and made the very existence of Jews in the Arab countries untenable. Was the final outcome a blessing and salvation to the Arab Jews or was it a curse? Was this really the final happy ending or would there be another chapter in the years to come, something more in keeping with the tragic history of the Jewish people? The debate was often heated. Other prisoners of war and other Israeli officers often joined in the polemics and Dr Abdul Salam had to act as a translator, conveying to the Israeli soldiers what their captives were saying, and translating to the Arab prisoners what their Israeli captors believed. Hassun and Abdul Salam talked about everything with the exception of one subject: Samira bint Haj Nufal and her final fate.

But not for long.

It was a fine spring evening in Israel, with the birds singing their good-night chorus and the roses and carnations drenching the air with their fragrance, when a Palestinian friend of Abdul Salam Sassoon brought him a bottle of arak, the potent Middle Eastern spirit distilled from grapes or dates, which was a favourite drink among the Iraqis. The doctor wanted to make a celebration of it. He prepared a salad of fresh lettuce leaves, minced red radishes, minced onions, sliced tomatoes, black and green olives, all tossed in wine vinegar and virgin olive oil.

Tiffaha cooked them grilled lamb's liver, kidneys and kebabs. It certainly was a feast. They ate, they drank and sang al-Kubbanchi songs:

Habibi la tadhin al-dahar sarna,
Hijarna diarina wa lilgharub sirna.
Wa hayatak ma dhihar lilnas sirna,
Lakin dam'i fadhahni wa 'amm aliya.

My beloved, think not that fate was kind to us,
We had to abandon our homes and drift westward.
Believe you me, I did not reveal our secret,
But alas, my tears exposed our tale.

It was almost midnight when Abdul Salam put his instrument aside. Hassun's eyes were bloodshot and moisture trickled down the fine grooves in his cheeks as he emptied the last drop of arak from his glass. He turned his head towards the older man and the words long held back flew out of his mouth, 'Dr Abdul Salam, I don't know why I fraternize with the man who killed my sweetheart, my Samira.' As he said this, he broke into a fit of crying like a child and put his head on the shoulder of Abdul Salam.

The doctor held him tight until the young prisoner of war recovered and wiped his tears and the slime from his nose with his hands. Abdul Salam handed him a box of tissues. He looked him straight in the eye. 'Hassun, I did not kill your Samira. She is still living somewhere in your country, probably in Basra.'

The revelation shook the the young prisoner to the

185

core. He legs trembled as he raised his head and let out a deep shuddering gasp of anguish. He felt as if his chest was going to burst.

'It is true, my dear. I didn't kill Samira but her parents don't know that. Now, listen. I pretended to her two brothers that I killed her and disposed of her body. But I just couldn't do that. How could I? She was such a lovely girl. I waited for her to recover from the anaesthetic and nursed her for two days. Then I took her with me to Basra where I entrusted her to the care of a good friend, my old colleague, Dr George Malik. I knew him well from the days of our training. He was a senior consultant at the Royal Hospital of Basra. He promised to find her a job in that town and look after her.'

'You mean she is now working in that town?' queried Hassun, taking in the implications of the doctor's words despite his agitation.

'Yes, as far as I remember. I asked him about her and he assured me that she was still working as a cleaner somewhere in Basra. I don't know exactly where. I didn't ask him. But you can go to him and ask him yourself. Karim, the taxi driver in Kadhimiah, knows where George lives.'

'Dr Abdul Salam, you have no idea how I feel. You did not give life to Samira only, for now you give it to me. For years I thought she was dead and that I was responsible for her death. But when I called on your clinic in al-Sadun, why didn't you tell me?'

'I couldn't because the moment her brothers learned that I had cheated them they would finish me off. They would ransack the world from China to Honolulu to find me and kill me. Such is the Arab spirit of vendetta.'

His eyes gleaming with joy and excitement, Hassun threw himself on Abdul Salam, hugged him and showered him with kisses, before darting out of the surgery without even saying good-night.

He rushed back to his barracks with elasticity in his cheerful steps. He radiated alarmingly high spirits. It was dark but for him everything was gleaming with promise and delight. It was not a prison. 'How could it be, when it is the place where I have learnt that Samira is not dead? She is still living and working in Basra. Oh, bless that city which embraces and sustains my beloved. Why did Abdul Salam Sassoon keep this secret from me? Why was it a secret? Was it a crime, a sin, an offence to keep a young woman alive? Should I hold it against Abdul Salam? All these days playing backgammon with me, singing of love together and yet suppressing this vital information. Was it the Jew in him, unwilling to help a Gentile? But he risked his own life to give life to a Gentile woman. Maybe it was Israel. A good Israeli must walk with suspicion and prudence, must keep the Arab in mental darkness, must not meddle with the affairs of the Gentiles.

'What is she like now? Does she hate me and

despise me for causing her all this misery and then running away? Does she hate all men now? I wonder whether she has formed a relationship with some other man, someone stronger and more determined. Oh, would she? I shouldn't blame her. She has had to build a new life for herself.'

Debating one point or another, Hassun spent the night, a smile on his face and so many words on his tongue and his lips, words which he mouthed but could not yet give voice to.

'Quiet, please,' hissed his neighbour in the next bed. 'You keep turning over and making a noise. Aren't you going to sleep?'

'Sh . . . sh . . . !'

15

Back on a Camel's Back

Dr Abdul Salam Sassoon walked to his surgery as usual, but for him to find a prisoner of war waiting for him so early in the morning was unusual – and it was none other than young Hassun Abd al-Ali.

'Dr Abdul Salam, I want your help,' said he, after making sure that no one else was within earshot.

The doctor went slightly pale and looked worried. His lips parted company and remained wide open for a few moments.

Hassun waited for them to close before opening his own mouth with a slight tremor. He looked into Abdul Salam's anxious eyes. 'I am sorry to come to you so early in the morning. I just couldn't sleep the whole night. Please don't repeat to anyone what you said to me yesterday. Now that I know the truth, I can't wait until we get repatriated. Believe you me, even one hour is too long for me. I must get to Samira before something dreadful happens to her. She may commit suicide. Her brothers may discover she is alive and go to Basra to kill her. I want your help, doctor.'

'What kind of help can I give you?'

Hassun looked around again before answering Abdul Salam. 'You must help me to escape from this detention camp. Please! Please!'

'Oh, Hassun, you want to get me into trouble? You have no idea.'

'Yes, I do have a good idea. You did a very courageous thing in the past to help Samira. Do it once more for her. Just one more act. Hundreds of Christians risked their lives in Europe to break the law and help the Jews escape from the Nazis. Please, Dr Abdul Salam!'

Gradually but steadily, young Hassun managed to win the doctor over. 'I suppose I can refer you to the Hadassah Hospital in Jerusalem for a further examination. The guards will be less strict there. You will have only a few hundred metres to cross to reach the Jordanian border. Israel will be more than pleased to see the back of you. One fewer Arab mouth to feed. You will need to get to Basra as soon as possible. Go to the Khadhimia district and look outside the shrine for a taxi driver with the name of Karim. Ask him to take you to Dr George Malik's house. He knows the place. It will also be cheaper and safer to go by cab. If you go by train you will have to bribe the military police. They will ask you for your documents. Well, well, old George will be stunned to hear this story from your own mouth, and he will be so pleased.'

With all the necessary medical papers prepared,

signed and stamped, the prisoner of war was to be driven with military escort to the hospital – but not before Dr Sassoon had slipped into his pocket two hundred-dollar bills, 'You will need something for your fares and the bribes.'

'I'll never forget what you have done for me and for Samira. How can I repay you?'

Abdul Salam Sassoon held Hassun by his shoulders. 'You know, Hassun, what I am dreaming of? One day there will be peace between us. I mean between the Israelis and the Arabs. I am as sure of that as I am of holding you now with my own hands. Jews and Arabs will be friends again as they always were in the past. I tell you, there will be a time when the Jews will forget their Farhud and the Arabs will forget their Deir Yassin. I have a dream. One day I shall visit you in Baghdad and see you with Samira. I owe her an apology for what I did to her. We shall sit on the Abu Nuas Corniche and drink together to peace in the Middle East. Yes, Hassun, and one day you will bring her to see us in here in Tiberias, a free man not a prisoner of war.'

The two men kissed and hugged each other for a while until Hassun had to tear himself away and go to join the military escort to the hospital. Once there, he contrived to evade his single guard, leave the crowded hospital waiting-room, cross the few hundred metres of no man's land and surrender to the nearest Jordanian soldier, waving a white handkerchief. But what he thought would be the trickiest part of his adventure proved to be the easiest; he was escorted by the sentry to the officer in charge of that section of the old city frontier, only to be arrested by the officer as an Israeli spy. The more he protested in his perfect Arabic the more convinced they were that he was a spy. Only foreign spies speak good Arabic. Like all sailors in trouble, he changed tack, and spoke to them in the English language, which he had learned from the Jesuit fathers at the American Baghdad College. He paid the price of his expensive education by having to endure four days of interrogation coupled with horrendous torture.

'Yah, he sure is a tough Zionist.'

They beat him up, hanged him from the ceiling upside down, twisted his arms, kicked his balls and tried all the usual forms of torture popular among Middle Eastern counter-espionage organizations. It is true, however, that Intelligence bosses tend always to behave contrary to expectations. Just when Hassun had decided to give up and pretend that he actually was an Israeli spy and hope for the best, the interrogation officers decided that he was not a spy. They apologised to him and asked him to sign a document to say that he had been well treated and had not been subjected to any torture or indignities. To top it all, the officer kissed him on both cheeks, gave him some bandages for his broken nose and some ointment for his dislocated shoulder and saw him off the premises.

'I wish you well, my brother. Long live Iraq.' Hassun limped into the street and crossed the road to get as far away as possible from the Security Department. From a pavement peddler he bought himself a new vest and pair of pants, khaki trousers and a shirt of the same colour. He walked back to the hotel, looking behind him all the time.

After three days lying flat on an iron bed in the al-Surur Inn in Saladin Street, he had recovered enough energy and physical mobility to go out and look around. The gentle air of the Jerusalem morning breeze refreshed his spirit and encouraged him to make the splendid walk around the old city and view its Ottoman gates. Outside the Damascus Gate, or what was called locally Bab al-Amud, he sat on the marble steps for an hour watching the crowds of Palestinians on their daily business in and out of the old city, selling oranges, confectionary, green olives, pinkish-red pomegranate juice and freshly cooked falafel. Orthodox and Catholic priests in their habits passed shoulder to shoulder with Muslim imams in their *jubbas* and Naturi Karta rabbis with their long black braids in their gaberdines.

Hassun's walk inevitably took him to the Noble Sanctuary of al-Haram al-Sharif. It was time for the afternoon prayer, to which he was invited by the custodians. His exhausted legs welcomed the idea enthusiastically and he could not refuse. He sat on the mosque's prayer carpet and let his thoughts carry him. He still had a major challenge ahead of him. How to cross the border and reach Iraq without documents. He prayed to Almighty Allah to show him the way.

In the afternoon, he strolled along the Via Dolorosa's winding lane to the Holy Sepulchre, where he sat on the front bench in the nave and made a similar prayer to the God of the Christians. Surely, he thought, one of them would answer his prayers and his plea for guidance. On leaving the church, a few beggars stretched their hands towards him and his negative answer to their prayers was brusque. Having paid his dues to the Almighty, Hassun caught the bus travelling to Amman. He took a service cab from there to Qasr al-Burque, some ninety kilometres from the Iraqi border.

There he stopped. How could he go any farther without getting arrested once more? Qasr al-Burque was a desert village with a few inhabitants and visitors mainly from the Badiat al-Shammar, a semi-desert area. With their long black braids and kohl-rimmed eyes, the Iniza tribesmen who straddle the border areas between Iraq, Syria, Jordan, Saudi Arabia and Kuwait look fearsome as well as handsome and picturesque. They aroused Hassun's interest, as he aroused theirs. With his right hand on his long studded dagger, Sheikh Abdul Razzaq Abu Isa, their tribal chieftain, stopped to ask him, 'You don't belong to this area, do you? Your aren't one of the king's men either.'

'No, you're right. I am just passing through, God willing, to Iraq, to my home town, Baghdad.'

Hassun's answer strengthened their curiosity. Like most people living in border areas, the inhabitants of this semi-desert expanse were practised in cross-border dealings, be it in smuggling contraband drinks and tobacco, sheltering outlaws and army deserters from one country or another, or conveying messages and intelligence. Before finishing his cup of bitter Arab coffee at the primitive local café, Hassun was able to fix a deal with them. For twenty dollars, they would offer him full board, so to speak, and see him across the border safely. The full board was based on two meals a day of yoghurt, dried dates, barley bread and coffee. He packed up his shirt and trousers and exchanged them for a Bedouin *dishdasha* and a rope for his waist. He looked just like one of them, even more so after a couple of days as he allowed his beard and moustaches to grow freely under the red *keffiyeh* which he wrapped around his head in the typical Bedouin fashion of Transjordan. The only difference was in the shoes. His were a rubber pair which helped him in mounting and dismounting his camel easily, which impressed the desert beast immensely.

To avoid the most fearsome rays of the desert sun, the march started early in the morning from the outskirts of the Jordanian capital in the direction of Qasr al-Azraq, then the camels veered southwards towards al-Hazim. The following day Hassun realized the sun was beating on his back. 'Where are you going? This is not the direction of Baghdad.'

'Don't worry, my son. We seek water and pasture for the animals. We are heading to Jabal al-Druz.'

'But the Druze are in Syria.'

'Be calm. Plenty of time. God willing we'll be there before sunset. It is only a stone's throw from al-Azim. Plenty of time,' Sheikh Abdul Razzaq assured him. The vast distances in the desert are made to seem short, a mere stone's throw to the inhabitants, by the clever device of conversation. 'Shall I carry you or will you carry me?' asked the sheikh.

'How can I carry you or you carry me when we are both on our mounts,' answered the young Arab.

'What I mean is,' said the older Arab, 'will you do the conversation or shall I.'

On this occasion, Sheikh Abdul Razzaq did most of the carrying.

'You think so? You think the Arabs will unite into one big happy family? But I tell you, my son, you must first get the tribe of al-Awaly to unite with the tribe of al-Lawaly and stop killing each other.'

'This will happen in time and with good education.'

'You mean there will be a time when a man from al-Ugaidat will not object to his son marrying a woman from al-Umayat?'

'They are not objecting to their sons marrying an English woman or a German woman.'

196

'That is different. These are women of Europe. They are not women from al-Awaly or al-Lawaly.'

'They have to learn that an Arab woman is as good as a European one.'

'You think so? But I tell you this. When we were under the Ottoman Turks, our people used to fight among themselves with swords and spears. We got rid of the Turks and our people started fighting each other with guns. Get them united and you will have them fighting each other with these new atomic bombs. What I say is get an al-Awaly to marry an al-Lawaly and the other way around, get a tribal chieftain to marry the daughter of a blacksmith and then think of uniting our Iraqi brothers with our Egyptian brothers.'

A young guide on horseback interrupted the debate to tell them the news from Jabal al-Druz was not very promising, so Sheikh Abdul Razzaq had to eat his words and order a change of direction towards Harrat al-Rujaila. 'Be calm, my son. It is only a stone's throw. God willing, we'll spend tomorrow night there.'

There was plenty of water and green pasture in Harrat al-Rujaila, which meant staying there for a whole week before marching southwards in the direction of Tarif in Wadi al-Sarhan.

'Where are you going now? We are heading south towards Saudi Arabia,' protested the young man.

'Be calm!' answered Sheikh Razzaq. 'Don't worry! It is only a stone's throw from here. We'll be there tomorrow.' He had scarcely finished these words when he observed a cloud of dust obscuring the horizon and moving towards them. 'The army!'

Two military vehicles with mounted machine guns trained on the camel caravan approached. Everybody stopped, which meant the camels were pulled up short which apparently they didn't like. They growled and grunted and his almost threw Hassun from the saddle.

'Everybody dismount!' said the commanding officer. 'You are smuggling guns into Iraq.'

'Oh no, officer. By Allah we are not. Search us!'

And search they did. They had all the luggage and baggage unloaded and opened. True enough they found no guns but they uncovered packs and packs of contraband cigarettes. 'I see! Smuggling cigarettes from the Zionist enemy. Very nice, by Allah! Working for the Jews, aren't you? You are all under arrest, men and women. You and your camels and your goats.'

The little problem had to be tackled discreetly. Hassun was trembling with fear. Soon they would discover his identity and it would be mightily difficult for him to prove this time that he was not an Israeli spy. The brilliant Sheikh Abdul Razzaq took the young officer aside and slipped into his large pocket twenty of Hassun's dollars. The officer's tone changed immediately. With a pleasant smile on his face he shook hands with the sheikh and wished him a long and prosperous life. 'May Allah Almighty bless your women with fertile wombs and ever flowing

198

milk.' The vehicles roared and disappeared behind a cloud of yellow dust into the depths of the wadi.

'Hassun, my son, this was all on your account. Somebody in Amman from the accursed tribe of al-Ugaidat saw you and tipped off the army about you.' Hassun took the hint and responded by compensating the sheikh accordingly.

The caravan resumed its progress towards Tarif and pressed on the following day over the Iraqi–Jordanian international frontier and on towards the small town of Rutba. Sheikh Abdul Razzaq led his men and his animals eastward to avoid the Rutba checkpoint and landed Hassun, as promised, somewhere along the main highway towards al-Rumadi.

'Thank you for your help. Now I'll be able to find my Samira.'

'What? Samira?' echoed Sheikh Abdul Razzaq Abu Isa in digust and disaproval. 'You took all this trouble for a woman? By Allah it is true what they say about you. You townspeople are all mad. You are a clever lot, but you allow your women to run your lives.'

Hassun climbed the embankment and there was the wide tarmac road extending in a straight line like a black ribbon on a yellow garment from the flat western horizon far into the north-east. It only remained for the young man to thumb a lift from one of the trans-desert vehicles on its way towards the town of Falluja, across the Dilaim Plateau and the old iron bridge over the Euphrates Valley.

❦ 16 ❧

The Blue Shanashil House

Everything in the Middle East revolves around the army. From it all living things come and to it all the dying return. Hassun Abd al-Ali had left Baghdad in a military vehicle and returned to Baghdad in another, as he successfully managed to get a lift from a military convoy returning from duty in Jordan. Yes, he thought, modern means of communication, even when military, are plainly more congenial than travel on a camel's back. He stretched on the floor of the tank carrier and slept all the way to the iron bridge of Falluja, some eighty kilometres to the south-west of Baghdad. He lifted his head and looked at the murky, yellowish flow of the bold Euphrates, loaded with mud and human refuse. Here and there, the bloated corpses of dead animals, black, sickly white and greyish brown, drifted away like giant toy balloons, carried by the waves from side to side in a southerly direction towards the sea. The air was steaming hot and the loathsome vultures were hovering overhead, waiting for someone or something to die and offer them a feast. They could see that the man on the tank carrier was not yet ripe for eating.

'Where do you want me to drop you?' shouted the driver. 'I can't take you all the way to al-Rashid military barracks. You are not a tank.'

'No. God forbid. I'll jump out at al-Khir bridge. I'll take a taxi from there. Thank you all the same. Long live the Iraqi army.'

Families are such a peculiar institution. The less you are in and the more you are out, the more you are appreciated and heartily missed. No sooner did Hassun alight from the taxi and knock at the front door of his parents' house than the whole neighbourhood heard the ululation of his womenfolk. Sayyid Abd al-Ali cried copiously as he hugged his son and showered him with prickly, wet kisses. Hassun enjoyed a whole week of generous hospitality and lavish entertainment from his friends and kinsmen before taking the bus to al-Kadhimiah to look for a certain taxi driver, the same old Karim. He jostled his way through the crowds of worshippers outside the magnificent golden shrine and soon managed to find his man.

'Yes, sure. I remember Dr George's house well enough. A very nice Christian he was. We ate there with Dr Abdul Salam and his madame. A lovely kind of fish. I mean the Shat al-Arab *sabbur* fish.'

The arrangement was made for Karim to call on Hassun early in the morning of the following day and together they would hit the road southward to Basra. As Hassun sat next to the driver, which he always did, he noticed a little portrait of a handsome woman fixed on the dashboard underneath a religious verse, 'Such is the bounty of the Almighty.'

'Karim, who is the damsel in this portrait, your wife or a film star?'

'My wife, thanks be to Allah and al-Kifil. When I travelled with Dr Abdul Salam to al Kifil – the Jews call him Ezekiel – I prayed to him in the mosque. I asked him to give me a scholar wife, one who could read and write. I made my prayer and forgot all about it. But one day, while I was taxi-ing, I picked up a passenger from the al-Majidi Hospital. She was in a terribly distraught state. I tried to console her and raise her spirits. She told me that she was Jewish and her parents wanted to take her with them to Israel. That was why she was crying. She loved our country and didn't want to go to Israel. One word led to another, and I proposed to her there and then – for she didn't know how she could stay in this country, a young woman by herself. I took her to al-Kifil and the sheikh married us on the spot. She is an educated woman and can read and write. She can read even the thermometer. She is a nurse.'

'A wonderful story!'

'Her name is Rachel.'

'Look after her.'

'She looks after me well. Jewish women make good wives and good mothers.'

Karim did not finish his story but broke into song

as he often did. He touched the photograph gently with the tips of his fingers and raised his voice.

Bint al-Chalabiah,'ayunha loziah,
Bahibbik min Qalbi, ya qalbi,
Inti 'aynayah.

The daughter of the merchant, with eyes
like almonds,
Oh my heart, I love you, my heart,
You are the apple of my eye.

Karim was astonished and puzzled that his passenger knew so much about the Jewish doctor and his madness. Hassun told him nothing about his captivity in Israel and the chance encounter with the doctor.

They arrived late at night in Basra when the entire city was shrouded in mist and smoke. They booked rooms in the Shat al-Arab Hotel overlooking the vast river of that name. It took the driver a couple of hours, the following morning, to find his way to Dr Malik's house where disappointment awaited them. Nobody answered the knock at the door, however much Hassun went on knocking and trying the bell, which was almost certainly dead. The house was as silent as a mortuary. No sign of any life was there other than a whole family of kittens feeding from the mother cat, who looked at the human intruders menacingly. The lawn was overgrown with weeds and littered with debris. Karim went around and knocked at the door of the neighbour's house to enquire about Dr Malik.

'Oh, Dr George Malik left for America months ago. He got his papers and emigrated to the United States.'

'Do you know his address or telephone number in the States?'

'Oh, we wouldn't know. We were not on speaking terms. He was a thorough rogue and seduced our Indian maid. The hospital may know where he went. They may be able to help you.'

That seemed a good idea. They took directions from the man and headed to the Royal Hospital of Basra, but again they drew a blank. No one could give them any information about the whereabouts of the gastroenterologist consultant, George Malik. Apparently, because he was not allowed to leave his post on account of a ban on the departure from the country of any medical practitioners, Dr Malik had been forced to leave his house with everything in it, including his precious violin, and his country secretly by crossing the river to Iran, just as Dr Sassoon had done. Iraq was no longer a land for those with an artistic or intellectual temperament. The erstwhile colleague of Dr Malik's at the hospital could tell them nothing more.

There was a pause during which Hassun turned his face up to the heavens. Cold sweat was breaking through the pores of his forehead and his forearms. But he had to try one last desperate throw.

'I am sorry to press you so hard but this is a matter of vital importance to me. Do you know of a young woman with the name of Samira, whom he might have brought to this hospital.'

'A rather handsome young woman? She was employed as a cleaner here in the Royal Hospital but she left us quite a while ago.'

'She caused a lot of problems here,' they were told by a youngish clerk in the hospital office. 'Sorry we can't help you any more in this matter. She went suddenly and without leaving us with any address.'

'Thank you all the same,' said Hassun, gritting his teeth to master the pangs of frustration. All the efforts he had made, his captivity in Israel, the long days of wandering in the desert and the endeavour and expense of coming to Basra were wasted like clean water poured into the sewage of Cairo.

He left the hospital office but he was followed by another young clerk who had listened attentively without saying a word. 'Excuse me, sir,' said he as he caught up with him. 'Did I hear you mention the name of Samira?'

'Indeed I did.'

'What are you to her, may I ask? Are you her brother or a relative of hers?'

'No. Just a friend.'

'Well, I'll tell you. But please don't be shocked by it.'

'Go on. Don't worry.'

'You may be able to find her in the Blue Shanashil House. I am sorry to say that, but I warned you about it.'

'What is that? The Blue Shanashil House?'

'Oh, I am sorry. You don't know it? I see you are not from this town. The Blue Shanashil House is a house of ill repute, a house for fallen women, a brothel, sir, if you'll pardon the expression.'

'Are you sure? This is indeed a shock to me. But I thank you all the same for this piece of unhappy news.'

'I am sorry, sir.'

Hassun felt his whole world crumbling. The tears trickling down his cheeks were but the merest indication of the horror he felt in his heart. He walked towards Karim's cab with faltering steps. They followed the route described by the young clerk to the Blue Shanashil House in the seedy part of the city, the Manzul area with its bars, nightclubs and whore houses.

'The women will be tired and sleeping now, Hassun. Best thing for you is to come in the evening. At least she will be at her best,' said the driver.

No. Hassun's heart would not allow that. It would break in the intervening hours. He knocked at the navy-blue front door, gently at first and then loudly. A peep-through grill, no bigger than ten centimetres square, opened. There was behind it a tired eye, smudged with traces of stale mascara. But no sooner did the eye appear than the grill opening was slammed tightly. Hassun did not know what to do next. He could feel his heart thumping harder and faster. His belly contracted with a swirl of emotions and the urge to pee seized him. In this state of agitation, physical and mental, he had no option but to repeat the same exercise, and this time to knock at the door with even greater urgency. The peep-through grill opened again. The same eye appeared, bewildered and shining with moisture, but then the grill once more closed tight.

'Look, Samira, Samira,' shouted Hassun hysteri-cally, 'open the door, please. Let me have a word with you, just a word.'

When Dr Abdul Salam had entrusted Samira to the care of his friend, Dr Malik had found her work in his hospital. But the circumstances were unbearable for her. As soon as they discovered that she was a fallen woman who had lost her virginity, every man, and woman for that matter, wanted to have sex with her. From the top directors and senior consultants to the lowest watchmen and sweepers, males and females, all had a fling with her. What she was giving for free, she could and should do for money, so she reckoned – with perfect logic. Wafiqa Khan, the well-known procuress, who was always on the lookout for just that type of pretty young woman, did not take long to discover Samira and offer her better employment. For a hundred dinars, she pawned her body to Wafiqa Khan and bought from her a bed, a pillow, a jug and a set of crude cosmetics, consisting of a lipstick, a box of powder and a pot of kohl. This hundred dinars the young man had to pay back to the madame to release his girl from her commitments.

The sordid truth was what Samira had to confess to Hassun in a tortured voice and with hesitant words as she snuggled into his side on the back seat of Karim's cab, with tears in her eyes and both hands clutching his hand. Hassun had to listen and endure what he heard as Karim was driving the couple to Basra International Airport. They were due to catch the first airliner to a foreign land – any foreign land where a woman does not get killed or raped for simply falling in love, let alone for making love, with the man of her choice.